Opposite of Collision

Opposite of Collision

A Novel by
Richard M. Timberlake

PALMETTO
PUBLISHING
Charleston, SC
www.PalmettoPublishing.com

ISBN: 979-8-8229-3835-9

Contents

Foreword

This story is fiction. The time period is the early-to-late '90s, when cell phones were a new thing, Bill Clinton was in the White House, and Princess Diana was still alive.

This story follows the path of two men from very different backgrounds: Randall Betts and Munir Afridi, two ordinary people who choose a path of service and sacrifice. Although their sense of duty and dedication belong to different directions, they are fearless and open-minded in their quest for acceptance and personal success.

Each chapter in Part One begins with the varying sensory receptors we sometimes take for granted. Although they become second nature to some and minor distractions to others, they are universal to us all. They are the *animalistic human qualities* that unite us as a species.

I hope you enjoy this story. It is a tapestry of different cultures and societies.

Prologue

The sidewalk traffic in front of the outdoor seats of this local tavern was the same pace and appearance as it had been for weeks—weary men and sad-looking American women trudging in front of the table service area. As it had been for weeks, the same bland population paraded in a methodical, nondescript sea of nonbelievers, those who should be taxed, converted to Islam, or put to the knife.

As Hafez Al-Zedicki watched them, he truly believed that the latter option was favorable to the others. These were pathetic, struggling peasants unaware of their destiny to face death and destruction at the hands of superior warriors for the Prophet. As Al-Zedicki looked past the stream of commuters, he searched for the skyline across the Hudson River to look upon his most recent effort to inflict pain upon the American culture. He looked at the symbol for all these thousands of meaningless people: the outline of the twin towers in New York City. Soon these buildings would collapse into one another, and the world would know of the true fatwa against the West: that anyone who did not subscribe to the teachings of the Prophet would never live their lives in peace and success. This was the bounty for the true believers, that those who believed that Jesus Christ was a conduit to Allah would pay or perish.

After an hour past the agreed-upon time, Al-Zedicki strained to see the tower collapse, but it was still there. Perhaps a true believer had been thwarted, perhaps the explosive charge had been inept, perhaps the van driver had shirked his responsibility and run away before the charge could be detonated. The plan he had worked so hard to prepare called for the towers to fall, and yet they were still there.

Then Al-Zedicki heard the news broadcast. A tremendous explosion had occurred under the North Tower of the World Trade Center in New York. Reports were thin at this point, but it appeared that several people had been killed, dozens injured, and the New York City Fire Department was still investigating the source of the blast.

Still investigating the source of the blast? What happened? The blast should have decimated the tower garage, allowing the weight of one tower to collapse into the other, bringing about the destruction of the most important symbol of the Zionist enemies of the Prophet.

As Al-Zedicki watched the news footage of ambulances and rescue personnel clearing out the garage of the North Tower from outside the café, he swore an oath that he would see to this monstrous building's demise. One day, he said to himself, he would make the self-righteous crusaders pay for their persecution of Muslims throughout the world. Anywhere the Westerner would stand, the Muslim would be there to strike him down. As he could hear the wail of sirens across the span of the Hudson River, Al-Zedicki left the outdoor tavern and waved for a cab to take him to the airport.

Part One

Chapter One

1100 hours, 27 February 1993
Badia Region of Jordan, seventy miles west of the capital

The most coveted form of sensory input is eyesight. The belief that for something to be believed it must be seen is a timeless lesson for humans. As modern, sentient beings, humans have come to rely more and more heavily on what they see above all else. The advent of computer-generated imagery has created many dichotomies for recent generations, as those who *witnessed* events created by keyboard experts were convinced that what they saw was real.

Randall Betts was a true realist. His time in the military and his reliance on science for examining on his own terms had convinced him that real life was something to be embraced. He never focused on video games or exciting action films to educate him; his preference was for learning and educating himself through his efforts and sometime failures.

He never relied on physical fitness manuals to tell him about his limitations. Swimming hard and fast in a chlorine-drenched pool with a squad of guys trying to stop you while pushing a volley ball between your arms toward a net twenty yards away told him how to control his breathing, how to focus on his target, and use his entire body to achieve a strike on the other team's goal. In short, Betts learned to use all of himself, not just his eyesight, to succeed.

Now Betts used his keen eyesight to look down the line of recruits at the shooting range. This was a group that relied on their uniforms to show unity rather than discipline or pride. These men were reported to be regular Jordanian military troops, young and inexperienced, and they were tiring of the routine of standing up straight and aiming their pistols at a cardboard target. The uniforms they wore were the same fabric, the same color, with the same single patch that signified their attachment to the Jordanian army, but the slumping, disinterested visage of these recruits was disheartening to Betts.

As a young marine lance corporal, Betts had signed on to a newly formed detachment, the Fleet Anti-Terrorist Security Team (FAST). The FAST mission was to create a small, well-trained cadre that could respond quickly to a wide variety of challenges and emergencies overseas. From supporting Embassy security teams to small-unit tactics in hot zones, this effort was a chance for the US Marine Corps to get into the *little* fights, and if it cheated the US Navy SEALs, out of a mission, well, the investment was worthwhile to the corps.

Based at the Naval Weapons Station in the Hampton Roads area of Virginia, the pace was lively but constrained. Betts yearned for some action, and when an offer had come through for a certified small arms instructor to support a CIA effort in combating terrorism overseas, he jumped at it. Little did he know that it was an underfunded project to collaborate with a friendly country to help train entry-level troops in basic firearms skills and ambush tactics.

Very blasé and rudimentary, thought Betts, but it got him outside the continental US (OCONUS) and gave him a chance to see how other militaries trained their people.

"At the sound of the beep, draw your pistols and fire two rounds into the target. You will have five seconds. When you hear the second beep, holster your pistol," came the command from Betts. His voice was sharp and clear. Even though the translated message from the Egyptian-born interpreter was less enthusiastic, Betts's voice command made the seriousness of the drill evident.

The pistols being used were worse than outdated; they were Helwan Brigadier Model 951 9-mm handguns, which were crude copies of a Beretta design from the 1950s. These items were made in Egypt at least thirty years ago, and the dull finish and numerous scrapes proved to Betts that these had not been holstered or well cared for. They were all-steel guns, weighing over three pounds each, and even in their advanced age, they were clumsy and stiff. They were housed on each student's side in cracked leather holsters older than the students, with a spare magazine stuffed into a pouch at the front of the holster.

When Betts raised his small blue box and pushed a button, a beep emanated and the drill began. The beeper ticked off five seconds and beeped again, signaling the end of the simple shooting drill. To Betts's surprise, three of the ten recruits on the firing line had already holstered their pistol, four of them were still trying to aim for a second shot, and the other three were finished, holding the loaded pistols straight down along their sides and turning to look at the instructor. This remarkably unsafe stance was more than simple ambivalence; it disregarded the safety of everyone at the range. As Betts shouted commands at the three men to holster their pistols, the interpreter began to stammer in Arabic, making the others undertake some measure of response. This created a short period of panic that took several minutes of repeated instructions on firearm safety and proper range procedures.

The interpreter, an aged man of about sixty who had been a doctor in a previous life but took the job as a translator as a way to make better money, approached Betts and spoke in a quiet, almost conspiratorial tone.

"The men are just a bit nervous as they learned earlier about a royal visitor to the training camp!"

Betts stared at him.

"A royal visitor? I wasn't told anything about this!"

"They just learned about it today," came the weak response from the interpreter.

He had arrived two days ago when the promised interpreter, a young officer from the Jordanian Special Forces, had been unable to attend the training. This last-minute substitution had been disappointing to Betts, but the local CIA Station Chief had assured him, "the old guy's okay."

"Why didn't you tell me about the visitor?" Betts asked, his temper beginning to show. This camp, a training base described as an old military storage site used by the Jordanian military for keeping expired and surplus materials, was being repurposed for joint military exercise training and secure operational planning.

The truth was that this *secret training base* was formerly a trash dump for the Royal Jordanian Air Force (RJAF) dating back to the late 1940s. It was about 115 kilometers west of Amman, in the high desert plateau near the Syrian border. After the six-day war in 1967, the RJAF had abandoned the space, returning only to dump more trash or dig through the rubbish that had been piled against old F-104 Starfighter aircraft for the potential of finding spare parts or avionics wiring. When an agreement had been signed between the Jordanians and the Americans, a defense-services contractor was hired to use bulldozers to push the trash into linear piles and cover them with desert sand. These piles, eight feet high and forty feet long, were then marked with stanchions and distance markers to create a shooting range of fifty yards down to ten feet. Betts and three CIA counterterrorism case officers were then dispatched to Amman as a show of partnership with the Hashemite Kingdom in their efforts to combat terrorism in the region.

The students liked to shoot from the ten-foot marker, but the smell of the trash, even under several feet of desert sand, made shooting from there for any length of time unbearable.

Today, as Betts stood under hellish sunshine behind the line of ten students at the ten-meter line while trying to stay calm in a swirling hot wind of dust and sand, the interpreter sheepishly answered him.

"These were just the rumors of young boys. And besides, if the impending visit of a member of the royal family was true, it would be a state secret unbearable by me."

As Betts prepared to tacitly launch into a quiet tirade against the old man's inability to coordinate with the team that hired him, he heard a familiar voice behind him.

"Randy! Straighten your shit! You have an audience!"

Betts turned to see Jeff Bovian, one of the CIA *instructors* who had been sitting in the air conditioning of the main office near the base entrance. Since the training evolution here had begun three days ago, the CIA case officers were happy to see to the administrative duties of the course and let the Jarhead do the actual training. After all, the marine was a certified instructor, and the agency employees were trained to spot, assess, and develop potential recruits for the agency. They did their work when the students were relaxing and more talkative.

"Who is it?" called Betts, pulling off his Sordin Pro-X ear protection and wiping the grit from his safety glasses.

He was caught off guard by the sudden interruption of the rudimentary but essential training drill. These recruits weren't just young; they were a bit scruffy from living in tents (no barracks here, just the range and a classroom created from cutting windows and doors in a forty-foot shipping container) and trying to improve their skills in a difficult environment. They were not exemplary troops, and this was not a premier facility.

"Some lower-end royal with his goons and a girl. Just show 'em the flag," Bovian said with a smile.

This meant that Betts should provide a cursory tour of the meager facility, introduce the students (he didn't know any of their names), and brief the visitors on the grand plans to shape these troops into well-trained fighters against extremism in their country. This was mostly bullshit, but Betts had been briefed that this temporary training evolution would pay great dividends for both countries. Bovian had more experience in the operational field than Betts, and he never failed to make that clear. Bovian had been placed in charge of this project, as the foreign-training office he worked in had been given the chance to make this work.

Bovian was slightly shorter than Betts, but his Ivy-League education and personal relationships with senior CIA officials made him a person of much higher station than others in his pay grade. Bovian wielded considerable sway, and this assignment to the foreign-training office, while meant to be two years, was simply a thirteen-month stepping stone to more important assignments.

As Bovian turned back to the main entrance building, Betts could hear car doors slamming and noticed a cloud of dust that had risen over the entrance from the approach of several vehicles. They had already arrived. As he looked beyond the entrance building, he could see that these were brand-new four-wheel drive Mercedes SUVs, all black and caked with dust. Whoever these people were, they were important.

Betts then turned to the interpreter, and found that he had started back in the direction of the main entrance building, following Bovian. Betts quickly stopped him with a curt call of his name and instructed him to advise the students that they were to unload their firearms, holster them safely, and proceed to the covered range. The interpreter did this in a rush, making it sound like an urgent command.

When the students started to jam their weapons into the aged holsters, Betts held up both of his hands in a signal of stop, then quietly informed the interpreter to emphasize to the students to clearly check their weapons to ensure that they were empty and safe, then carefully holster their weapons and slowly make their way to the covered range. Betts knew the basic rule: never run on the range, and never rush to make a weapon safe. The interpreter got the message and slowly enunciated the instructions in a parochial and childlike manner. As Betts was set to remind the interpreter that he worked for Betts and not the other way around, one of the students called out in good English, "We got ya, boss! Safe and secure!"

Betts looked to see that it was the second-youngest soldier in the group. His comment elicited laughter from most of the other soldiers, making it clear that they understood English. All but one was smiling. Betts noted that this soldier didn't speak English well.

The covered range was reserved for rifle fire, as the course of fire for rifle training included shooting from kneeling and prone positions. It was a thirty-five-meter range, with one of the trash berms on the eastern end; three long plastic folding tables on the western end, where students could lay their rifles and ammo; and no walls north or south. This range had been created by knocking the walls out of a decaying aircraft hangar and leaving just the roof supports and roof left over. This would make a better presentation area for the visitors, in that it was out of the sun and would allow some shooting (if necessary) in a safe environment.

Betts stood the line of students on the far edge of the folding tables and had each of them unholster their pistols and lay them on the table. Betts stood on the other side of the table, separated from the students by a good three feet but placing himself between the giggling students and the VIPs at the main entrance building.

After assembling his students in some sort of a straight line (they were all craning their necks to see who was visiting this desolated place), Betts briefed them quickly and made sure that the interpreter did his job efficiently and quietly. Betts had been through VIP visits before. When he was a young marine, a congressional delegation (CODEL) had visited the Naval Weapons Station to see firsthand about this new *antiterrorism* team. Betts and his squad had been warned that any uniform not clean and straight or any unkempt living quarters would result in revocation of a weekend pass and a quick assignment to latrine duty. Just as the gunnery sergeant was finished with his *briefing* to everyone in the platoon, one private asked if any questions could be directed to the visitors. The steely look in the gunny's eyes was a glare that Betts could see even though he wasn't looking at the man.

"You say one word that I do not command you to say and you will be flayed," he said.

While many of the others did not know what the word *flayed* meant, they simply presumed that gunny had used the word *filleted*, and they received the message just as well.

As Betts turned his attention from the gaggle of students (keeping them in line was just impossible) to the back door of the main entrance building, he saw a group emerge with Jeff leading them onto the concrete pathway that led in the direction of the range. The back door was about fifty feet from Betts's position, so he could make out good details of the visitors, three of whom were listening to Bovian drone on about *his* program and the unique opportunities afforded by the US.

The group paused just outside the back door and stood together in polite attention to the briefing. Most of the visitors, serious-looking young men with varying degrees of olive complexions, appeared to be about six feet tall, fit, and dressed in the same cut of suit. One of the group, the sole male visitor without a mustache, was translating Bovian's boasting. This drew the interpreter to scurry from Betts's side so he could introduce himself and undertake answering any questions the gathering may have. In all, there were five males, four guys dressed alike in sharp black suits and ties and one male in a dark blue suit of a much better fabric and fit who was doing most of the talking. Betts presumed that the four identical black suits were security men and that the better-dressed guy was the VIP.

But wait, Betts said to himself, the VIP doesn't do all the talking and translating. He was just above six feet tall with a slender build, wore a better suit, was clean-cut, and a much better haircut than the others, but he was interacting with Bovian and the others like he was a regular guy. Didn't make much sense.

And then he saw the girl. She emerged from the far end of the group as they walked from the main entrance building. She was the last in the line and had huddled around the group to hear more of what was being said. She was just over five feet tall, wearing a green and gold silk scarf over her hair and a thin white sweater over an iridescent beige dress with gold piping at the seams. And she was gorgeous. Even at that distance with the arid swirling air and the generous makeup so popular in Middle East culture, Betts could see her bright beauty and contrasting vibrancy. She was in a class completely separate from the group. Betts surmised that this was the VIP, not just *some girl* that Bovian had described earlier.

As Betts was soaking in the light of this woman, he heard a new sound and it made him turn quickly. He didn't want to appear anxious or distracted to the group of visitors, even though they were fifty feet away and listening intently to Bovian, but the sound was wrong, and he needed to address it. As he turned, he realized the sound was from one of the students dragging an empty 9-mm pistol from the plastic tabletop and inserting a full magazine into the pistol's mag well. He fumbled only slightly at getting the metal magazine into the bottom of the grip, and Betts recognized instantly that it was the student who had not laughed at the earlier statement, the one who didn't speak English well.

As the magazine slid into the Helwan pistol and locked into place, it made a distinct sound that ranged between the click of a door lock and the slam of clanging metal. When this sound was heard, two things happened: the other students fell away from their gaggle and went to the ground with a scream of terror, and Betts grabbed the edge of the folding table that lay between him and the student.

The pistol was quickly raised, aimed at the VIP group, and a quick shot rang out as Betts pulled the table up with all his strength. Just as the tabletop emptied of the other pistols and made contact with the student's body, a second shot fired. The impact of the table pushed the student backward, but the full force of the folding table was diminished by hitting the other students lying on the ground. The first sound of the pistol being picked up from the top of the table to the table crashing into the lone standing student took just over two seconds.

Betts lunged toward the shooter, raising his hands in the air to block the student's view and pushing himself off the ground as best he could from a high, crouching stance. As Betts tried to emit a distracting scream while in midair, he could see that the student had lowered his pistol from the high-ready position and was retracting it into a level that was pointed straight at him. The next shot would go directly into Betts's midsection.

But the backward momentum and Betts's exaggerated jumping and screaming had caused the student to lower the heavy, ancient pistol too far, and the edge of the folding table caught the wrist of the student's hand that was holding the gun. It came loose as Betts made full contact with the student, and they crashed heavily to the dirt. The dead weight of Betts's 190 pounds on the slightly smaller man knocked the wind out of the student's body so completely that his yelp was hardly heard by anyone but Betts.

Betts tried to compose himself and revert to his USMC training.

"Disarm then disable; no sense trying to whip an armed opponent!" he remembered.

Betts scuffled his right hand down the student's left side to determine where the gun had fallen, while holding his left hand tight on the student's throat. In the ensuing struggle, Betts could see that the student was suddenly alive with gripping and twisting and turning under his instructor's weight. It was incredible to Betts that, for the better part of a week, this student had been slow to react to instruction and lazily clomped around the range. But now he was a wriggling mass of hatred and violence.

Betts could barely contain the determined struggle of this young man, even though he had had the wind knocked out of him and had the stronger man's hand at his throat. He could feel the student getting out from under him and the table that laid between them. Possibly this young man had done some wrestling or judo training earlier? His scuffling and violent writhing had just about pushed Betts off him, and the loaded pistol was not yet found.

Betts made one last lunge to his right to locate the pistol when the student made a surprisingly forceful push with the right side of his body and ripped himself from under Betts . As the student struggled to get to his feet, Betts reached out to grab the man's wrists and hopefully control him. Their struggling and grunting in the dirt and dust of the covered range hampered the sound of the screams coming from the VIP group behind him. Betts was focused now on simply getting a good lock on the shooter, rendering him unable to get to the pistol. But the student had raised to a low crouch now, held down only by Betts's hold of his wrists. Betts was still flat on his side and was reaching up with urgency and tenacity against an opponent who was coming to his feet.

Then Betts heard a voice behind him that he didn't understand at first, a gasping, forceful voice that consisted of two languages coming from the same person,

"Got him boss! *Waqqif!*"

The shooter suddenly halted his resistance and became completely still. His eyes of searing hate and determination changed to dismay and fear. Betts could feel the other man's body become rigid but not resistive. Upon hearing this strange voice behind him, Betts found himself holding the wrists of a man in complete surrender.

Betts turned to see the student who had earlier called him *boss* in perfect English, standing just behind him with the loaded 9-mm pistol in his hands aimed directly at the man who ten seconds earlier had been a classmate.

"It's okay now boss, we got 'im," he said, and the student repeated the loud command of *stop* in Arabic to the shooter.

Now Betts could barely hear the other shouts and screams coming from the area of the main entrance's back door where the VIP group had been standing. As he turned and rose to his feet, he instantly became terrified at the sight. Two of the black-suited visitors were advancing on him and his students with guns drawn and aimed directly at them. And these weren't outdated handguns with scratches and faded bluing. These were polished Beretta 92Fs that glistened as the pair advanced and screamed commands at the group.

Betts instantly raised his hands and shouted, "Okay! Okay!"

He added all the Arabic words for *safety* and *yes* he could remember. But the two armed men continued to edge forward together at a clipped but frantic pace. It seemed that no matter how much he and the other students screamed that they were in compliance, these new shooters, these men sworn to protect the royal family at all costs, were not standing down. Just then they were joined by two other black-suited men carrying H&K MP5 submachine guns with the stocks extended and tucked tightly into their shoulders, also aiming at the group. These men were coming at them, guns raised, ready to kill.

Betts then turned from the advancing men to see the student who had been shooting, the one he had fought so hard with on the ground, standing in exactly the same spot as before. He was completely still, in a low crouch with his hands raised just above his shoulders and a look of abject terror in his eyes. Six feet away from him, just behind Betts's right side, the student with the gun stood completely still with his weapon still pointed at the shooter. He wasn't going to let him run away or be shot in the back and become a martyr for his cause.

Betts quickly understood that this student's motivations were valid, but he was going to get himself (and potentially a lot of others here) killed in the crossfire.

Ignoring the screams of the security men, Betts leaped to his feet with his hands held high. He then turned and dropped his hands to grab the arms of the shooter, and they collapsed together once again to the ground. At this, his English speaker dropped his pistol and raised his hands, which resulted in the security men demonstrating a high regard for discipline by instantly dropping their aim and holstering their pistols. The two men with the submachine guns dropped the aim of their weapon but remained in a shooting stance, ready for any change in the situation. Betts saw none of this, he just laid on top of the shooter, gripping his arms and drawing his arms back until he could hear the man scream. Then Betts felt the sudden, violent hands of one man pull him to his feet as another zip-tied the shooter's hands behind his back.

Betts could feel the man holding him as the shooter was pulled to his feet by several of his students and roughly led away, and Betts turned to see that it was one of the security men holding him. Betts relaxed his body enough to allow the security man to release his grip. Once Betts was completely free of the security man, he felt the man's grasp return to his arm as he made several statements to Betts in Arabic. Betts couldn't make out what the man was saying, but somewhere in the long paragraph was the word *shukran* (Arabic for *thank you*).

At that moment, Betts found that his hearing was slightly impaired. He could hear what the man was saying, but it was almost completely drowned out by a ringing in his ears. Evidently the sounds of the pistol shots very close to Betts's head had turned down his eardrums a bit, and in all the excitement, he had barely noticed it.

He looked over to see his English-speaking student complete a set of commands to two of the security men holding the submachine guns, and they hustled off as though their lives had been threatened. The student now approached Betts, who gratefully shook his hand and feigned a look of dismay.

"The bodyguard wants you to know how much we appreciate your bravery and quick action," the student answered.

"Five seconds ago they were going to shoot you, and possibly all of us in the process!" said Betts.

"They were reacting to the shooting; they were a bit scared and were trying to protect the prince."

The student continued. "In this uniform," as the student pulled on the lapels of his BDU blouse, "they didn't recognize his brother."

"You're the prince's brother? You're a prince too?" exclaimed Betts, suddenly becoming lightheaded from all the input and ringing in his ears.

"My presence here was not to be known, but I wish to add my thanks and gratitude for your efforts."

"My efforts? You saved my life!" said Betts.

"Do I still have to refer to you as boss now?" said Prince Ali Hassan Majid of the Hashemite Kingdom, third in line to the throne.

"Do I have to refer to you now as Your Highness?"

The two men laughed and walked together to the main entrance building as frantic radio calls could be heard from the inside.

Chapter Two

Two weeks later
Basement of CIA Headquarters, Langley, Virginia

Many books and training courses have been created in an effort to sense when another human being is lying. Many of these views and *scientific* studies have been welcomed as truths, when in actuality, the truth is that telling a lie is an organic response specific to the person telling the lie. Nobody can truly detect a lie if the other person is comfortable lying, and the signs and detection strategies built on *catching* someone in a lie is, at best, a suggestive dialogue. Only the truth can expose a lie, and for many of us, the truth is extremely elusive.

Randall Betts sat in a windowless office with very few decorations, a desk, four chairs, and a low table. Betts sat in one chair near the wall, and an attractive woman in a yellow cotton dress sat in the chair across the office from him. The third chair was empty, and the fourth chair, the one behind the desk crowded with papers, charts, and a massive computer monitor, was the chief of Liaison Training, the CIA officer that had sent Betts on this training mission. His name was Mike Chaffees, and he was a former football player at the University of Pennsylvania (Betts knew this from the sole picture of him in uniform on the wall), and a former civics professor at the University of Maryland (Betts knew this from the lone ceramic plate on the low table).

Betts had requested to come to CIA HQ for a brief discussion about the *shooting incident* that had occurred at the training facility two weeks earlier. The USMC had welcomed Betts back from his *detailed assignment* with the agency by issuing him an Article 15 nonjudicial punishment letter, referred to as *Office Hours* in the Marine Corps. Betts fought this administrative action as best he could, explaining that he had not shot anyone and had not caused the shooting. Hopefully this meeting would clear up the matter and result in a letter to his commanding officer clearing him of any wrongdoing.

He had been escorted into Chaffees's office by a very friendly man of advanced age, and now he sat in this windowless room in the basement, wearing a red *V* badge (for uncleared visitor) and waiting to hear anything positive.

"Randall, this woman is with the Office of General Counsel for CIA," Chaffees said to get the meeting started. He intentionally did not give her name.

"Pleased to meet you ma'am," said Betts.

"Corporal Betts, you allege that you had nothing to do with the shooting that occurred at the training site, correct?"

"Yes ma'am. I tried to prevent it from happening."

"Yet in your statement issued to both the CIA and your command, it was clear that you allowed live ammunition and working firearms to be present when the shooting death occurred," she stated with a coldness that shook Betts awake.

"We had been notified of a VIP visit while undertaking live-fire training drills, and all I could do at that time was to have the students clear their weapons and holster them just as the VIPs arrived, ma'am," replied Betts.

"Stop calling me ma'am," she shot back in a polite but terse voice.

"Sorry, but all you'd have to do is ask the locals. They'll tell you that there was no time to completely secure the firing line before for VIP group arrived!" replied Betts in a slightly emphatic manner. His defensive posture was growing, and he stifled the urge to shift his posture to face her.

"We haven't heard anything from the Jordanian government," Chaffees cut in blandly.

"What? We were sent there to train them! How can they not have said anything?" Betts was starting to sweat now.

"They will not confirm any travel plans or locations of the royal family, and any security matter is under the purview of the Mukhabarat (The Jordanian Security Service)."

Chaffees was backing off any responsibility for this, and this statement hung in the air as Chaffees and the OGC lawyer stared at Betts.

"Well, what did the other instructors say? They must have reported this in official cable traffic!" Betts was now pleading for some semblance of sanity.

"Jeff Bovian submitted his report in an Eyes-Only cable to senior management. Even I haven't read it," said Chaffees with a hint of withdrawal. Now it was time for the lawyer to chime in.

"We don't dismiss your account of the events, Corporal Betts; we simply find that some mistakes could have been made..." She smoothly cooed, but Betts cut her off.

"Damn right! The mistake of allowing an assassin into a secret training site as a student, resulting in that old man's death is a hell of a mistake!" Betts was now turned in his chair hissing these facts into the face of the OGC lawyer.

The sole casualty that day was in fact the interpreter. As he was standing between the visitors and Betts's students, he was the one hit by the second shot fired by the shooter. The first shot had (naturally) gone high and shattered a window on the main entrance building. The second shot, fatal to the interpreter, had penetrated his chest, but the spinning bullet had changed course inside the thin, wiry body of the man and emerged from his shoulder, just behind his collar bone and wedged into the overhanging fascia of the building beyond the visitors. Whatever the appearance of the Helwan pistol was, it was an accurate and effective firearm.

"As we've tried to tell you, we don't have any verification of a student who fired those shots that day. The security service will not confirm any arrests or terrorist events that day."

She was making the effort to calm Betts, but it wasn't working. Betts was coming to his feet.

"Well, you have a dead translator and some holes in a ramshackle building from a thirty-year-old handgun that nobody carries anymore! I was hustled out of that country so fast I didn't have time to clean up, and the airport security screening didn't detect any gunpowder residue on me. It wasn't me who shot the guy, and it wasn't a suicide, so you figure it out." Betts concluded this rant by walking confidently out the door.

"Corporal, you'll have to be escorted out. You have a red badge," called the lawyer in a parochial manner.

"Then you'll have to catch me. MA'AM. And that's lance corporal!" called Betts over his shoulder.

"Think he's telling the truth?" Chaffees asked once the hallway outside his office was clear.

"I don't know. He seemed pretty defensive. The cable Bovian submitted doesn't absolve him of any responsibility," the OGC lawyer said in a cool, dismissive manner. She had read the cable, but was more inclined to find fault with the military guy with the poor manners rather than CIA officers.

"Yeah, his CO says this whole mess resulted in him leaving the marine corps and going back to college," said Chaffees.

"Good. Maybe higher education will teach him how to behave in a civilized world," she said as she rose to return to her office overlooking the forested greenery of Northern Virginia.

★★★

After a frantic search for a staircase, Betts finally found a door that led to the ground floor of the expansive headquarters building. As he walked out, he handed the badge to the Security Protective Officer (SPO) standing guard at the side entrance he had used earlier. "Excuse me sir, where's your escort?" called the SPO.

"Call the OGC!" called Betts as he pushed through the outer doors and felt the warm sunshine on his face.

Chapter Three

5 April 1994
Birir Valley, Chitral District, Pakistan

Of all the efforts to communicate well, speech is the one that allegedly passes on the message from one human to another best. But this is a misnomer; it is actually the nonverbal communication that conveys the message, whether intended or not. The use of symbolism, color, fabric, or even timing of the nonverbal message can pass along a lot of information to the receiver. Whether perceived or not, the issuance of nonverbal communication can be a powerful addition or disruption of the spoken message, and we as humans must trust the nonverbal message over the spoken one.

The Birir Valley of Chitral District in northwestern Pakistan said a lot of things about its inhabitants before anyone could speak with them. As Hamza Khattack eased his large frame out of his Range Rover and trudged into the small hamlet at the edge of the Valley, he was struck by the clear beauty of the region. He walked along a bare pathway that had been used by old trucks and horse-driven carts, and the lack of tall vegetation in the crown of the pathway was due to the goat herders who allowed their flock to keep the grass short.

Khattack was here on business, but the clear mountain air and moderate temperature made him wish he could stay longer. The sole detractor of the lush, green valley that laid before him was the sight of the residential housing that blighted the landscape. These people chose not to simply erect a one-level house on the ground and use a mud wall around it as everyone else in the Federally Administered Tribal Area (FATA) did. They built elaborate, brightly colored homes of various materials and textures onto the side of the mountain. To these people, building vertically rather than horizontally ensured protection from both the elements and the manmade threats. This was madness, as a simple storm or shake of the Hindu Kush mountains on which these peasants had built would bring down their homes. Khattack was unsure if this had ever happened; the government of Pakistan would refuse to step in and help, surely, but he was certain that they had failed to expand their hamlets due to this short-sighted culture. It was of little matter to Khattack anyway. These were Kafirs, nonbelievers, who worshipped crazy spirits, and the sooner Allah would wash them away, the better.

Khattack was a senior intelligence officer with the Inter-Services and Intelligence Directorate (ISID) for the government of Pakistan. As an ISID officer charged with such responsibility, it was his job to investigate and report on any irregular activities in violation of provincial or Pakistani law. As his region fell within the northwest frontier province, he held large sway in these duties. His word was law in the eyes of the government, and as long as the Chitral district did not create any problems and paid their fair share of tariffs and duties imposed upon them, nothing undertaken by Khattack would be considered a problem.

But today was not a mission for the government; today was a mission for those who supplanted his salary in exchange for recruiting young men (and sometimes women) to assist in the great Muslim Jihad against Western tyranny. Getting volunteers from this region was rarely successful, as the people here were bystanders. They were content to let the rest of the world go to hell as long as they had their children and their crazy homes and their goats and their festivals. These people were the Kalash, a tribe of people thousands of years old, who were rumored in history books to be descendants of Alexander's army as he advanced through eastern Europe to northern Asia to plunder the Silk Road. His army had extended itself so badly in the Hindu Kush Mountains that many of his troops had stayed in place, resulting in a closed society in northern Pakistan that defied any other explanation. The Kalash people were not nomadic, they had no specific deity (they worshipped multiple gods), and the core of the population were blue-eyed with thick, blond hair. In the world of simple disciples of the Prophet Muhammad, they were neighbors to be abhorred.

Khattack walked on, careful to keep his clean white *shalwar kameez* blouse from becoming fouled by the vegetation. He had parked his Range Rover several hundred yards from the village and approached on foot, so as to appear as a guest and not an intruder. At his age, the walk was a welcome bit of exercise, but the years of desk work had rounded his figure to where he sported the belly and fleshy face of a true bureaucrat.

He finally came to a central house in the matted assembly of multi-family structures that these people called home, and politely announced his presence by saying hello in Pashtun to the man pulling grass in a small herb garden in the front yard.

The man stood stiffly and turned to Khattack. This man was Badshaw Afridi, and he was as purely Pashtun as any villager in the Northwest Frontier Province. He was 150 centimeters tall, thin and rigid as steel wire, with a beard beyond one handful and a high, shiny forehead above his steely gaze from light brown eyes. He regarded Khattack for a moment and returned the greeting in a traditional *Pashtunwali* style. Khattack was a guest and to be honored, until he wasn't.

"How may I be of help to you?" asked Badshaw.

"I have come to discuss some help that you might be to the brethren," came the smiling, positive response from Khattack. The straightforward comment proved that he was a man of purpose, of responsibility, of power.

Badshaw said nothing at this. He simply lowered his head, turned to go into his house, and called out one name. The name of his wife, Ashta Afridi.

Khattack was annoyed at this but expected it. These Kalash had no respect for Sharia law; they had no honor for the wishes of the man of the house. They chose to honor the female as much as the male. Badshaw had simply turned the matter of this visit over to his wife, and that began the most difficult part for Khattack: dealing with Ashta.

As Badshaw had left his guest at the front garden without a wave, Khattack could not venture further. He remained there, awaiting some attention from these peasants. With one phone call, he could summon three carloads of ISID agents and have these insignificant nonbelievers arrested or shot or both. But as the government lawyers in Islamabad had passed a law preventing any discrimination against the Kalash people, this routine practice was now frowned upon.

Soon enough, Ashta Afridi appeared at the door and looked over Khattack with little regard or respect. She was typical Kalasha—brightly colored panels of various fabrics knitted into a heavy sweater over a blouse that was black with various stripes of red, blue, purple and yellow stitched onto the edge of the sleeves. Her gown was similarly colored, and she wore sturdy leather sandals. Ashta's long hair, light brown and thick, was piled high on her head, with some evidence of being pushed into place. This indicated that she had been out earlier in the day and had worn the traditional Chitrali hat. But not now; she was less than keen on being outside her home.

But the feature that stood out was her eyes. Ashta did not have the bright blue eyes of her tribespeople; instead, she bore the mix of blue and light gray that made her gaze something to be noticed. She was a strong, handsome woman in her forties, and she fixed a gaze on Khattack that was at once sharp and focused. Her posture showed that she had little respect for this fat spy agency wonk, but her eyes conveyed that she added hatred to the mix.

"Ashta, I have come to speak with your son about a great opportunity that improves his education and shows him the world," said Khattack with a sincere tone of generosity.

"You want him for your crazy Jihad so he can die at the hands of some Russian pig!" She spat. She had lost Azzam, her firstborn son to this Islamic idiocy, and she was determined not to lose Munir, her youngest to it.

"No, this is not across the border. This is a chance for Munir to see Europe and North Africa, maybe even America," Khattack countered with an enthusiasm that created some stir inside the house behind Ashta.

"Has Hafez Al-Zedicki made you that rich that you can offer such foolishness? He'd never get past the Khyber Pass before you'd sell him off to bandits and thieves." Ashta was aware of such things; she knew of the foreign terrorist leader Al-Zedicki and his twisted fatwa, and neither her son nor her adopted son would fall into that trap.

As Khattack raised his hands in protest, a young boy appeared in the doorway behind Ashta. This was her adopted son, Hamid. He was Pashtun and dressed as one. He never adopted the appearance of the people that saved him from being stoned to death by his own family.

When the Mujahideen had come to Chitral Valley in 1982, looking for volunteers to fight the Godless Western Invaders in Afghanistan, Hamid's family signed up quickly. They were not true believers, but as Pashtuns, they had a duty to fight any aggressor, and the Russians were the worst aggressor since the British. When Hamid declined to join his brothers battling these strange invaders, his family tried to kill him because of the dishonor he brought to the family. Only the intervention of Ashta and Badshaw Afridi saved him from being stoned to death in front of his village. Hamid was fleshy and stooped, in his early twenties, and had no formal education. Everything he had learned was either by mistake or from Ashta.

"Hamid, go inside," said Ashta, distracted by the boy's presence.

"I want to hear what he has to say," came a voice from the far side of the house. Ashta and Khattack turned to see Munir Afridi standing just beyond the small garden. He held a basket of fresh herbs that he was bringing to his mother.

Munir was taller than anyone there, almost two meters tall and weighed seventy-five kilograms. He had light-brown hair and light-brown eyes and had not undertaken to grow any beard, although he was over twenty-two years old. His shoulders were thin and wide, and his outfit bespoke of a traditional Kalash male, dark pants and blouse with red and blue stripes at the collar. The men of this culture dressed more for work than for show, but they always bore some semblance of color that set them apart from other Pakistani men. The Chitrali hat on his head was thick and pale, and he was looking expectantly at Khattack.

"I have travel vouchers for you and Hamid to fly to Peshawar and then to Karachi, and onward to the port and then all over the world! You will learn many cultures and languages," said Khattack.

"He speaks five languages now," interrupted Ashta. Munir had learned Pashtun, Urdu, Arabic, English, and some French. His mother had schooled him herself, and her knowledge of the world was the result of a modern education in Afghanistan that no longer existed.

"Mother, Hamid and I have talked about this kind of chance. We really want to travel, to meet others, to have adventures," Munir said hopefully.

"The adventures he's giving are in prison or death," said Ashta sharply.

"You live your life in isolation and dare to accuse me?" Khattack started to raise his voice. He had tired of this female Jinga-dressed peasant and her disrespectful protests. Khattack's venous tone made Ashta turn her attention from Munir to this fat spy pig before her.

"This is where you have wasted my hospitality," came a quiet, growling voice from inside the house. Hamid scrambled from the doorway to make way for his adopted father. Badshaw stood rigid now, facing Khattack directly but staying just abreast of the doorway. At that moment, Khattack knew that the man of the house had retrieved his rifle and had it close at hand. *Pashtunwali*, the ancient ritual of welcoming a guest, had limitations. And when this ISID agent raised his voice to the woman who bore him sons, the hospitality ended.

Khattack had a Makarov pistol in his belt and two knives in his boots, but his AK-47 rifle was left in the Range Rover. This would not be a productive response. Drawing the pistol required a very quick reach under his long blouse, and while killing the Afridi patriarch would be a pleasure, Khattack could not be sure that he could get a shot off before being cut in half by an ancient single-shot 7-mm rifle. The Pashtuns had survived thousands of years of war, invasion, and petty squabbles by being quick and accurate with any weapon available, and the invasion of the Russians had opened a treasure trove of options for killing. Khattack was prepared to challenge the old bastard, maybe get him to raise his long rifle so that it could be snatched from his grip and used as a hammer on his bare scalp.

"It's all right father," called Munir. "I want to go with him."

Badshaw continued to glare at the ISID agent, making it clear that he was still not welcome any further.

"Excellent," responded Khattack. "My car is just over the ridge. I'll be waiting. Goodbye to you both." And he turned away.

Thirty minutes later, the two boys had hastily packed a bag and were standing in the small kitchen of their home, looking at Ashta. She was standing over the stone hearth, pushing small chunks of warm flatbread into single sheets of clear plastic for them to slip into their bag.

"I don't know when you'll eat next, so be sparing with how you use the bread," she said in a low, sad tone. Her heart was heavy, Munir could tell, but she had several things to say.

His father Badshaw stood at the back of the kitchen, staring at her. He was more concerned with her state of mind that he was with the destiny of two young boys. Even though his son was one of them, his concern for her heartbreak was obvious.

"You'll keep this with you always." Ashta held up two identical small canteens. "Fresh water will sustain you, even when these evil men will not." She wanted to make them stay, command them to stay away from these shallow promises of travel and adventure, but Ashta understood that it was time for them to make their own decisions. Even if she disagreed with their decision, and desperately hated the men who offered this opportunity.

As the boys took them from her, it was obvious that they were handmade reminders of their homeland. Ashta had made these months ago; she started with two small bladders of thick plastic with a wide, covered spout. They were rinsed-out soup rations from an emergency-response program provided by UNESCO when Munir was a little boy. The rations were the sole food available after a devastating earthquake rocked the entire Northern Province of Pakistan, from Kashmir to the FATA. Ashta had treasured them over the years, and now she used them to help these boys survive. The plastic bladders were placed into multicolored wool patches and then stitched tight to keep the liquid protected from heat or cold.

She then sewed on a woolen rope about one and a half meters long, attaching one end of the rope to just under the plastic spout, and the other end to the far end of the newly formed pouch. In this way, the canteens would be carried over the shoulder like a small bag. It was simple and functional, but it was also beautiful and sturdy. This was the reminder of Ashta and the Kalasha. This would be the symbol that sustained Munir.

"Cool!" exclaimed Hamid "We can use these as slings against the Christian crusaders!" With this, Hamid roughly tucked his prize possession into the canteen between the plastic bladder and the wool covering, an old Polaroid picture of himself standing with Ashta and Badshaw, the people who saved his life.

The silence from this rude and uninformed statement by Hamid deadened the sound in the kitchen. Munir knew his adopted brother had uttered nonsense, and he knew Ashta's rebuke would be scathing. Instead, Munir heard his father speak for the first time in almost an hour.

"Your enemies will be closer than the crusaders, and your fate lies in the misuse of your tools."

This was Badshaw's paraphrasing of an ancient Pashtun saying. It was very appropriate at a time such as this.

Once the hugs and promises and warnings and prideful statements were done, the two young men hustled out the door and headed in the direction they had seen Khattack walk. They were gone, and the house felt the pain of emptiness.

Badshaw spoke first.

"So I shall have none to help me with the wheat harvest."

"You will do fine."

Ashta smiled and held the side of his sad face in her right hand.

"You will do the cutting, and I will do the gathering, and you will do the tying, and I will bring the cart."

With that simple sentence, she had organized the harvest of

almost three hectares of wheat that would sustain several families over the winter. The wheat harvest would also provide a small balance of money by selling at the local market.

This would be grueling, backbreaking work for weeks, in addition to the harvesting of nuts, berries, and assorted fruit that rounded out the diet in this region. Ashta knew that the results would be meager, but she could do nothing against it. This region had it's perils and it's pleasures, and the best she could muster would be the loving companionship of her devoted husband.

Badshaw was a true man; he was skilled in farming and in hunting, and he had always provided well for his family. His attention to his children, his affection for his wife, and his strong devotion to the village and its people made him a giant in Ashta's eyes, and he was the only thing that mattered now. His strength must be her strength. Later, as she knelt to gather basil leaves and dates for their supper, Ashta bent over in her small garden alone and cried.

Chapter Four

19 April 1995
University of Richmond, Virginia, Marsh Hall

The human ear can determine a certain tone of sound that means something important has happened. Mothers can hear it in the voice of their child when calling, and mechanics can sense a misfire in an engine's operation that helps them determine a potential problem. The frequencies for serious or calamitous sounds are different from those for laughter or upbeat messages, and over our lifetime, our ears are trained to discern the difference, regardless of our awareness of it. Animals can naturally discern such sounds as well because they depend upon their hearing to survive. Humans do not develop an awareness of such sounds because they normally don't need to.

Randall Betts heard that sound when he came back to his dorm. He walked into the old brick building by the side entrance because it was fewer steps from the new gymnasium to his room on the third floor. The television in the common area was blaring, and the crowd huddled in front of the screen didn't smother the sound. Even in the din of this largely unfurnished area of the dorm, Betts could hear the strange concoction of sirens and sadness in the voice of the reporter at the scene of some panic-stricken event. Betts was looking forward to getting his studies caught up before heading off for Spring Break, and the sudden rush of immediacy and discernment was distracting. But still he joined the crowd hovering around the twenty-four-inch television.

This sounded bad, and as Betts approached, he saw both males and females turning away in horror from the TV. It didn't even seem unusual to him that females were in the dorm at that hour of day.

After a minute of peering through the assembled dozen students, he eventually made out that the scene was in the capital of Oklahoma, and that a bomb had gone off. He knew something about Oklahoma City. He served with a marine from there who was always bragging about the oil and natural gas supplied by Oklahoma. Betts quickly assumed that a gas mainline or supply tank had exploded. It certainly looked that way to him; all he could see behind the reporter was building debris and burned-out vehicles.

Apparently, the word had gotten out to others (not Betts, who had been playing racquetball that morning) that something had suddenly happened, something horrible.

"What's going on?" Betts asked everyone in the room.

"Somebody blew up the Federal Building in Oklahoma."

"Who did it?"

"They're saying that Arabs were seen driving away before the explosion."

Betts began to feel drawn to the drama; he began to secretly want the camera recording other parts of the scene to start panning over to other portions of the exploded building so he could see more.

Upon seeing a better image of the blackened shell of the Alfred
P. Murrah Federal Building, looking like a large shroud standing
on its own over the scene, the terrible aspect of the bombing did
not immediately become clear. But as he watched, and the unend-
ing loop of damage and grief played again and again, the typical
questions of why and who became overwhelming. Betts found
himself watching more intently just to hear the answer to such
questions. Answers that never came. Either they were drowned
out by all the tragedy of a nine-story building blown up in the
middle of the eighth-largest city in the US, or they were too sen-
sitive to be answered.

"Man, that place was creamed," someone from the crowd said.
Betts recognized him as one of the players on the university's rugby
team, but now he was pale and held a perplexed look on his face.
He was in shock. They all were.

Betts had faced this kind of calamity before, both in marine
corps training and during brief interactions with the intelligence
community. He had sat through numerous slideshows of the bombing of the US Embassy in Beirut, and had practiced performing
rescue operations at a mock helicopter crash. So while his three
years in the marines providing force security and working postblast
investigations made him somewhat older and more prepared for
this sort of tragedy, the enormity and closeness of this bombing
made him begin to shake.

"Randall!" Came a familiar voice behind him, and he turned
just as his girlfriend Denise rushed into the room and hugged him
tightly, completely oblivious to the fact that her boyfriend was
soaking wet from his racquetball workout.

"It's horrible! All those people dead! All those children!"

"What children? It's a courthouse, right?" Betts was suddenly
aware of how little he knew about this story and became frustrated
that Denise knew more than he did.

"It's a federal office building, and they had a nursery on the second floor! Two dozen children were in that nursery, right on the front of the building, and they can't find any of them!"

She was sobbing and covering her face now, and her words disappeared into his damp sweatshirt.

Betts walked her out of the common area amid the mounting commentary about who did this and why and how badly the Arab terrorists were going to pay for this attack. They had perpetrated a horrible attack when he was training indigenous soldiers before, but this wasn't overseas, this was in the US, and they had stepped over the line this time. He couldn't be part of this discussion, not yet.

A month later, on May 4, Betts called his former marine corps commanding officer from a payphone in the university's commissary. His CO, Darryl Beeker, had left the corps to work for the FBI and was now tearing up the world working at the New York field office, the largest law enforcement center in the US. As they talked, Beeker sensed that his former lance corporal and platoon leader wanted back in, to take up the sword and get back into the fight.

"So what I'm hearing is that you want to leave all the polite society and start slogging your way through life again," said Bleeker warily.

Betts replied, "Captain, I don't want back in the corps, and I don't want to spend my life waiting for some asshole with a pistol to make a mistake. The job I did in the Middle East was ruined by extremists that used Islam as a weapon against us. And now we've learned that it wasn't foreign terrorists that tore up Oklahoma City, it was Americans! I'm convinced that this isn't the end; these foreigners now know they can strike inside the US bigger than the WTC bombing, and they'll be after us again. I want a job that will get me into the real fight, the ability to chase these bastards down overseas and get ahead of them."

Betts felt the tightness in his throat when he said this. The same tightness he felt the day the radio announced they had caught the American perpetrator of the Murrah Building bombing. The anarchist who drove the van that blew up the building was captured through a routine traffic stop in a nearby state, and he admitted the crime as a payback against the US government for their actions against fellow countrymen in Ruby Ridge and Waco.

"First thing, I'm not your captain anymore. So you can start by calling me Darryl. And you have my work all wrong. We are not just trying to outlive these guys; we are going after them hard, all over the world."

"That's where I want to be," Randy interrupted him. He had heard before all the ups and downs of working for the FBI, mostly from former marines who had joined the bureau. He knew he didn't want to be part of some huge office of type-A assholes with guns falling all over each other to make a name for themselves. And he didn't want to be standing on a range in the desert, hoping to avoid being shot by one of his students. He wanted a place where he could strive, thrive, and accomplish the mission with minimal feedback. He knew what needed to be done, and he wanted the chance to do it.

"Well, hold on there hotshot. You haven't graduated from that overpriced mecca of socialist isolationism yet."

Bleeker had graduated from an extension campus of a worldwide college and had little use for grand institutions that took in large amounts of tuition so that young people could misbehave in a well-manicured landscape.

"I'm going to raise my grades enough to get permission to take summer school and get enough credits to graduate in August."

"You what?" Bleeker stopped and stared into his phone.

"The school requires that juniors who have a good load of credits and want to graduate early have a 3.0 grade point average. It's their way of encouraging the achievers and discourage the fast-trackers from speeding into law school. I'm going for it. I've already talked to the dean of students, and he will support me."

"You've already made your mind up. And while I will never disapprove of anyone saving the US taxpayer an extra dime, I'm unsure what you need from me."

Bleeker knew that Betts was attending the University of Richmond with much of the tuition paid by the GI Bill. Big schools were eager for the tuition money, and the US government cared little about the outrageous cost, as long as the GI who took advantage of the benefits actually attended the school.

"I need a reference," Betts said, somewhat sheepishly.

Beeker said, "You've already told me you don't want to work for us."

"You have contacts in the community, don't you?" Betts asked without hesitation. He had been thinking about this. The term *community*, without having to say it over a nonsecure phone, meant the intelligence community. Betts still wanted to be a spook.

"Hoo boy, that again. Will you never tire of romantic attractions to arduous lifestyles?" Bleeker said as he rolled his eyes.

"The marines gave me that."

"The marines aren't giving you this. This is a real career choice, not something you do for a couple of tours and climb out. This is long, hard work."

Bleeker was serious now. This was a big step, and both men knew it.

"Do you know anyone? Someone I can talk to?" asked Betts, tiring of the discouraging talk.

Bleeker sighed.

"The local contact with the JTTF (Joint Terrorism Task Force) is not very easy to deal with. A real civilian who thinks terrorists exist only for exploitation. I know a guy at Langley who may be able to meet with you."

Betts thought he was doing the right thing all the way around. At twenty-six, he was older than his classmates, and his time in the Corps made him a bit more mature and a good judge of character. Pushing his posture to get a measurement of sixty-nine inches, he was shorter than most of the students, but what he lacked in height, he more than made up for in stamina and drive. He may have struggled to stand out among all the athletic kids at U of R, but he could hold his own in water polo and racquetball.

Overall, however, nobody would really miss him in school. He had made no real friendships outside of Denise, and his devotion to her more than made up for the lack of social contacts. Denise was everything to Betts, and he was sure of her feelings for him. While he had not thought about pushing the issue of marriage or a young family, this new path was going to necessitate some choices; Denise was a junior just like him, and she might not care for being apart from him for almost a year while he went into some secretive lifestyle. This would be tough to sell; he was unsure if she would support this.

What Betts was sure of was that his time of joyfully ignoring the rest of the world and thinking he was safe had passed. No longer could he simply choose between electives and burger joints and consider himself useful. Betts could not stay in the artificial world of academia, debating the relevance of religion or the paucity of political will to end hunger, while people were plotting to attack his country. He had attended a speech held in the university auditorium presented by a former navy commander who had been held hostage for months by the North Koreans because he and his crew were caught operating a US spy ship in the South China Sea. The speaker, a grizzled old salt who spoke with both dignity and passion, declared that the United States had decided after Pearl Harbor to ensure that the activities of foreign countries were to be discreetly monitored for the sake of national security. Naturally, students spoke out later that this speaker was an apologist for a corrupt, paranoid government that sought to control the world through spying and espionage. Betts thought differently—that the old man had served his country as best he could and that, when confronted with a tough situation, he had strived to protect his crew from further harm. That was a noble effort that inspired Betts to do his part, to take his turn in helping to make his country safe.

Chapter Five

4 May 1995
Ummar Farooq Mosque, Nowshera, Waziristan Province of the
Federally Administered Tribal Area (FATA), Pakistan, thirty miles
west of Peshawar

The sense of smell has evolved through thousands of years of evolutionary survival. The animal who can smell an intruder survives the incursion of an enemy. Relying solely on what you can see or hear may not guarantee safety, as these senses can be tricked by slow movement and camouflage. In modern times, mankind has overlooked much of this capability due to the lack of animal attacks and a more sedentary lifestyle. The sense of smell has been relegated to aromatherapy and shrouding the blandness of personal living space with perfumes and scented candles.

In the compound where Munir Afridi and his friends were being housed, the sense of smell was overwhelming. The tawdry smell of goats kept inside the compound walls along with the hot stench of burning trash made Munir wish for the clean mountain air he had taken for granted in his home village. But a more visceral smell was becoming clear: the smell of distrust. Slowly, Munir became more aware of the grand promises and controlled urgings of his instructors. The quick lessons and insincere smiles provided by tired, overweight men who rushed through the Quranic verses and weapons training started to paint a picture of manipulation. Munir assembled a private but nagging sense of smell that the grandiose visions of these *leaders* had more to do with an uncaring agenda than a sacred mission.

At the same moment that Betts was attempting to earn his degree quickly and join the CIA, 7,100 miles away, Munir Afridi was uncertain what the image on the screen was showing. In an unadorned room in the far left corner of the mud-walled mosque, across from the kitchen and back door, he and a group of other young men sat on the floor around a TV while a much older man pointed out details being shown from a VHS tape that had been smuggled by NGO workers through the Kyber Pass. The grainy image was frozen on the small television screen. The six young men leaned forward and strained to see what the instructor was pointing out in the center of the exploded hull of the Murrah Federal Building.

"You see here that the blast penetrated perfectly into the body of the building. The ends of the building are still standing, which indicates that a great deal of reinforcement was dedicated to these areas, but the center has collapsed from the sheer blast. You see this because the reinforced concrete could have sustained the weight. What caused this much blast penetration was the percussion created by the other buildings across the street. This helps increase the blast compression, thereby making a small bomb have much better results. We are currently seeking out similar locations where the Americans are located, so that we can take such advantage."

Munir leaned in a bit but not too far toward the screen lest he bump heads with the other men looking. The image on the screen demonstrated an incredible amount of destruction, and Munir wondered if anyone had survived such a blast. What the teacher was saying was technically correct, but the value of the information was chilling; why would they be trying to duplicate such damage?

Despite the fact that mostly policemen inhabited the building, this was a civilian target. How could this explosion have any value in a military sense? Munir wondered to himself what kind of people he and Hamid had become involved with. His goal was seeing more of the world than just the smattering of houses piled against the hills in his native Chitral, and finding a decent job wouldn't hurt either. Munir and Hamid had struck out from their families to explore the vast world beyond the jagged landscape of the Hindu Kush and obtain work that would allow them to return home and invest in their native culture. Munir saw this as a noble, almost holy, endeavor as his village suffered badly from years of isolation and governmental neglect.

Munir's Kalash background was something he diligently kept from the other people there. His heritage was one of ridicule and scorn in the northwest frontier province of Pakistan. Although he was the product of some of the most forward-leaning teachings of the Prophet, Muslims treated the Kalasha as something medieval that had to be brought *into the fold* of proper Islam. The Pashtuns regarded the Kalash people as some other tribe with strange values and practices, and that made them vulnerable to attack as outsiders (even though they had lived in the region next to the Pashtun for thousands of years). The calls of *Kafir* and *blondie* were insults Munir had heard before, and he didn't wish for that here. When the government of Pakistan stepped in to make it a crime to discriminate against the Kalasha and forbade the practice of converting them to *traditional* Islam, very little changed.

Hamid was also in this group and was trying to concentrate like his adopted brother Munir. Although he was Pashtun, he had grown up in Chitral and had known Munir all his life. Munir's family was a bit odd (especially Munir's Mom, Ashta), but they had stayed good friends throughout their school years. Ashta took Hamid in as a second son, and he had lived with Munir's family ever since.

Now as they sat side by side on the cold bare floor of the mosque, Hamid ran his fingers over the slight lump in his colorful canteen, the lump caused by the Polaroid picture of him with the Afridi family. He was grateful for the life they had given him, and he was proud of the canteen he carried over his shoulder constantly. The only question in Hamid's mind was why Munir had always kept the canteen hidden under his clothing. This was confusing, but Hamid brushed it away as he tried to concentrate on the teacher's lecture.

The teacher was trying to show the value of using the natural urban landscape as a means to amplify explosive effects of simple chemicals when mixed properly, and Munir was beginning to understand that these techniques would be useful in defending the Muslims who were fighting the *new nationalist enemy of Islam*, the Serbs. Now that the Serbs, Bosnians, and Croats were fighting for imperial control of huge sections of the former Yugoslavia, the Muslim brothers who lived there for generations and had helped settle this region were now being pushed and slaughtered by the nonbelievers. That is what Munir believed he was involved with. What other reason could it be? The preservation of Islam was the natural duty of any Muslim, regardless of the sect or alignment. Munir was beginning to see the big picture now; the lesson learned from the blast created by this American zealot would help him and the others attending this class better understand how to defeat the Serbs in Bosnia.

"Teacher, how did he get so close to deliver this bomb? Was he martyred in the killing?" asked one of the young men. Munir was curious as well but did not want to bring attention to himself.

"He simply parked the vehicle in between the vehicles and walked away," was the confident answer of the teacher, an elder from the Peshawar area brought in to prepare these young people for travel to Bosnia so that they could prove themselves worthy of further battles against the West.

"And he was not caught for doing this?"

"He was away before they knew anything! He served his cause and inflicted much damage to the autocratic government. He is a hero because he struck the enemy at their heart and survived to make his displeasure known!"

The teacher had chosen his words carefully for these young men. It was important that they see the positive side of fighting for Islam and the personal rewards that would follow.

As the group this teacher was working for had sworn an oath to a religious entity and not a state government, it would not be easy to convince volunteers to sacrifice themselves without a promise to reward the families. When recruiting young men to strike a blow against the Zionists or the occupying forces, it was easy to promise money to the family of any volunteer. This made ensuring a young man's devotion much easier. In the case of these young men, the teacher was obliged to show that fighting for Islam in Bosnia was a clear duty and the rewards were the triumphs themselves, whether the volunteers survived or not.

The teacher sighed as he answered another question about how soon they would be going to the action. He grew weary of his task, convincing these young men that their future was dependent upon their service to *The Base*. Although the leaders of this Sunni sect had plenty of money, they parceled it out in pitiful amounts and expected droves of young idealists to do their bidding. While the teacher knew that plenty of young men were available, and that it was easy to infuse them with hatred for the West, the truth that these men were being prepared for—either slaughter in Bosnia or suicide attacks somewhere else that Islamic *leaders* deemed appropriate—just seemed so...wasteful.

When the class was finished, the young men stood and thanked the teacher profusely for his words of guidance and wisdom. Munir was unimpressed with the old man, as his knowledge of the bombing was very shallow and the smell emanating from him was very deep. Deep, like in one of the pig pens in his home village. In any event, Munir had been taught early by his mother that respect for those who teach should always be high.

"Older than you by a day, wiser than you by a year," is what Ashta would always tell him. Well, this teacher had also skipped his bathing for a year, thought Munir to himself. Hopefully, the travel would start soon and Munir would get a better view of the world than the cold floor of a back room in a mosque.

When Munir and Hamid had been convinced of the great opportunity in Nowshera that awaited them, they were told that they would be trained as warriors who would wreak havoc in the Western world and punish the aggressors who sought to crush Islam and subject all Muslims to re-education in huge European death camps. The description of this mighty effort, spun by the traveling fruit salesman from Asadabad, made Munir and Hamid think they would be a new age form of Zoroastrian avenger, fighting their way across all of Afghanistan and Persia, arriving just in time to save the helpless Muslim brothers who were being killed and chased from their homes by the merciless Serbians. This effort would be quickly accomplished, as the Serbs were simply a vocal minority in the country where all the Muslims lived, and the rewards for such an accomplishment would be heralded throughout the world as men who stood up and fought for their religion. Munir felt this might improve the image of his people in the world, that the Kalash were responsible Pakistanis who helped protect the world. Maybe then, Munir thought, the

Pakistani government would do more to protect the Kalash from being wiped out as a culture in the Hindu Kush region.

After being here for four weeks, Munir had begun to feel differently. The squalor and poverty of this area was obvious, and the instruction he had been given—lectures on why the West should not be trusted, demonstrations of bomb assembly, and range instruction on properly firing an AK-47 (they never did show the right way; Munir knew from the teachings of his father)—had failed to convince Munir of the wisdom of this *crusade against the crusaders*. Even the hands-on instruction on the rocket-propelled grenade did not include actual firing of the rocket, just the instructions on how to fire it. A waste of time.

Naturally, Munir did not share this with Hamid. Hamid was loving all of this experience because it was time away from the poverty of his own village, and it was a chance to show his family that he was a true warrior. Munir knew that Hamid was ashamed that he had not followed his family into Afghanistan in 1982, and Munir had tried to tell him that he made the right choice. Indeed, Hamid's family had been all but wiped out in the first two months in Afghanistan when a Russian helicopter had strafed a mountain camp on the far range in the mountains just across from the Chitral Valley. They hadn't even made it to the fighting in Kunduz, Munir told Hamid, and his death would have ended the bloodline of Hamid's family. That made Hamid feel much better.

Now Munir and Hamid were fighting on their terms, taking on a godless foe in a foreign land. They would join other volunteers and travel to southern Russia (living right in the backyard of the aggressor) and learn from Kist veterans of the fighting in Yugoslavia, and then be flown to Turkey and march into Bosnia and take back the land for the Muslims. This was a grandiose plan that required an enormous amount of coordination and money, thought Munir.

As he wondered where all this money was coming from, Hamid rushed up with a fresh disk of naan.

"Did you hear that we would be leaving soon?" gushed Hamid, tenderly tearing off half of the bread and quickly handing it to Munir.

"Yes I did. My clothes are clean for the trip," Munir said as he hungrily tore into the warm, toasted bread. One of the great things about living here, thought Munir, was that the bread was almost as good as the naan made by his mother. He thought of her as he took a quick swallow of water from his brightly colored canteen and covered it with his tunic. This symbol of his homeland was all that remained for him, and he wanted to keep it safe. Once it was tucked away, he looked around the outside area where he and Hamid had sat to eat.

Across the small courtyard, through the smoke rising from the fire in the stone oven, Munir saw a man proceed from the back door of the mosque and cross to a small building. He watched the man intently as he walked purposefully through the others without acknowledging any of them. He stopped to say something to two strangers who had come in earlier in the day, but the man swiftly left them and proceeded into the building and shut the door. The two men glanced at each other and continued to sit quietly. Munir then reminded himself why he had watched this man so intently—he was someone to be avoided. Munir had heard stories about powerful leaders within the realm of Islamic Jihad, and this man was surely one of them. His determined gait and lack of fellowship showed him to be a man of purpose, but his eyes showed him to be that of a djinni, an evil spirit. Munir didn't know who the man was, and he was sure that he didn't want anything to do with him.

As they finished their midday meal of naan and dates, Munir became more apprehensive about the trip that awaited them. Was this man walking into the small building someone he would travel with? Was he the man arranging for the travel? Munir didn't know. As he had always been eager to see the world and make a name for himself, Munir had come to miss his family and his home. His mother and father had made a very comfortable life in the hills on the far side of the Chitral Valley, and although he had no brothers or sisters (his older brother had been *converted* to Islam and taken to Gilgit when Munir was very young), he regarded everyone in his village as family. Why would anyone want to leave a peaceful valley where all were treated with respect and nobody shirked from hard work?

Munir upbraided himself for being silly and selfish. The true path to honoring one's family was to be successful. And if the opportunity does not exist where one lives, then they must strike out to find that opportunity to succeed elsewhere. Traveling was something commonly done in the border region of Pakistan. Businessmen, imams, produce sellers, even average farmers all moved through the Old Silk route made famous long ago, from Kazakhstan to Waziristan. These trading routes were full of roads, taxis, buses, and all manner of transportation. Even some of the poorest people moved through the region by aircraft; Pakistani Air had aged planes flying through Peshawar all the time, a virtual exodus of refugees at any given hour of the day. In the case of this region, it was more than simple curiosity about the outside world; it was an important part of life to travel out and find oneself. And this is what Munir was doing, whether he was going to help win back the land for Muslims in Bosnia or interviewing for a job in Karachi, it was his obligation to his family to taste success.

In a nearby building in the same compound, Hafiz Al-Zedicki was completing his plans for moving these new recruits through Afghanistan to Kyrgyzstan, where a Georgian smuggler would transport them by freighter across the Caspian Sea to Armenia and then on to the Black Sea for another quiet boat ride to the port of Rijeka, Croatia. This industrial port, with its business dealings as murky as the Mediterranean waters that fed it, was the perfect place for overland transport to the Danube River where trucks would quickly transport them to the Muslim hamlet of Bihać. This pipe-line—over one thousand miles long and requiring the services of dozens of facilitators—was being stretched thin due to Al-Zedicki's constant need for fresh recruits for the jihad, but the reward from the sheikh was worth it. Any upbeat assessment or affiliation with a local attack (Al-Zedicki had learned to quickly take credit for any horrible crime in the name of Islam) would be welcomed with the acceptance of a local Hawala for additional funds. This was the way things were done in the careful world of transnational funding of terrorism: have a courier from the sheikh travel to a money broker, a Hawala dealer operating from a small but legitimate business, with news that a sum of money in local currency was being promised to another. That broker would be provided the money and then contact a money broker in the country where the funds were to be sent and advise them to pass the funds to a worthy recipient. Frequently that would be a courier not attached to Al-Zedicki's network, but he would accept the funds and pass them to Al-Zedicki through a cut-out. In this way, millions of dollars, pounds, shekels, and dinar were transferred throughout Europe, the Middle East, and the Americas with no actual money trail to follow and no records to illuminate the sender or the receiver.

It was a system as old as Islam itself, and it relied on the trust-worthiness of the vendor and the senders of the cash. The difference in this modern age was that much of this correspondence did not rely on in-person couriers as much, as the advent of cellular phones and the new form of informal messaging called *texting* put the message out in a much quicker manner. On this night, huddled in a building no bigger than the garden shed of most American homes, Hafez Al-Zedicki arranged for $12 million in US dollars to facilitate the transport of almost two dozen fresh recruits to the war against the Western oppressors. Troops that were necessary to prove to the world that this fight for Islam would not be ignored and preserve the supply of trucks, drivers, smugglers, and middlemen to keep this pipeline alive.

The next act conducted by Al-Zedicki was a call to a Saudi financier to ensure that the money that had been promised earlier would be forwarded to a small group of men in Lebanon. They would facilitate not just a local driver but also arrange for funds to be transferred back into Saudi Arabia for the purchase of a gas tanker truck for delivery of a huge amount of explosives. This simple action—a call to ensure that the money had been secretly transferred from Saudi Arabia into Lebanon and then back to Saudi Arabia—put a long list of actions and actors into play. It had taken months to prepare and would take another year of planning to execute, but it would be worth it. The United States would get a real taste of punishment for its policies, but this time it would not be from a bunch of nitwit American hermits, it would be from dedicated believers.

When he was done with his cellular phone calls (a modern convenience provided by rich telecom companies eager to make a profit in the impoverished districts of the FATA), he called for his two couriers. He provided fresh funds to the couriers and intently instructed them on the messages they were to bear in his name. These instructions were critical to his success, and the couriers repeated back to Al-Zedicki the messages several times to ensure they recalled it properly. No written notes that could be found at border inspections, these messages (and the funds) would put his plans into place and conceal any ties to him. Once they had left, Al-Zedicki laid over onto his mattress and feel into a deep sleep.

Chapter Six

10 December 1995
Vint Hill Farms, Warrenton, Virginia

The sense of touch is a sensation that has served mankind longer than recorded history. The nerve ending responses of texture and temperature have provided a semblance of both pleasure and alarm for the earliest hominoids, and modern mankind is no different. Even the advent of textures that are smooth or synthetic has not diminished the importance of the sense of touch. It is as important to the modern human as the sense of sight, even though they can be mutually exclusive.

In his townhouse just outside Warrenton, Betts was learning how it felt to touch something that rejected any sensation of acceptance or pleasure. His hand rested on the shoulder of his girlfriend Denise, and she had turned away from him as though his fingers were poison to her flesh.

"What's the matter? I thought you'd be happy for me to get an assignment overseas!" he said. He had invited her to travel from Richmond to his apartment so they could celebrate the good news of his being accepted for a temporary assignment in Europe.

"For you, maybe, but what about for us?" demanded Denise, who turned away from Betts and stared out the back patio door.

"You're going to be gone during Christmas? What do I tell my parents? How am I going to enjoy going home for the semester break with this hole in my life? Don't you care about how this assignment would affect us? What do they want you to do, kill more people in the name of US aggression in the world?"

The weight of this statement struck him so hard he could barely mount a response without stammering. When he tried to speak, she continued instead.

"So, you want to help Big Brother get more oil rights and weapons contracts?" Denise interrupted him. "You don't have to explain it to me Randall, I know all about these backroom deals to use internal squabbles to rush in and get favorable trading status agreements just so they can keep punishing the Russian people! The US won't stop until Russia gives up its oil and adopts the dollar as the sole currency. Face it Randy, you're just a tool for American aggression in a world that just wants peace. You're the same as the Aryan Brotherhood assholes, only you're the terrorist on the side of those who oppress everyone!"

Betts undertook his explanation, overlooking the obvious snub of his service to his country, "Denise, this is what I've been training to do. It's not a two-year assignment; I'll be back in three months. I'm going to be part of a multinational effort to help save innocent lives from the Serbs! These people are…"

"…Too poor to buy a US congressman to save them, so they throw in a bunch of knuckle-draggers to shoot it out and save democracy!" interrupted Denise.

The bland disregard for what was going on in the former Yugoslav republics was not unexpected. Denise's family had not been in the military; they had lived comfortably in the Northeast and considered the armed forces as goons and lower socioeconomic castoffs who were programmed to create chaos wherever and whenever the military-industrial complex instructed.

Betts countered with some emotion, "These people are pawns in a war waged by nationalists more interested in destruction than democracy! You saw what they did to the Olympic city of Sarajevo! It's gone, and a million people are refugees thanks to these thugs! And it's not the US hurting anyone; we're joining with neighboring countries to fight back and…"

Denise calmly interrupted, "Goodbye Randall, have fun playing with your toy soldiers; let me know when you're tired of world domination."

And she walked out, leaving Betts holding the TDY assignment forms that he had happily waved earlier. He looked down at his hands as he held them, trying to find some form of support or positivity in the standard USG papers, but they suddenly felt cold and hard and unable to empathize. He just felt alone.

Two hours later, as Betts finished his second drink of Blanton's bourbon and ice, a loud knock erupted on the front door. He was still in a deep funk of self-blame and personal recrimination, and the thumping on his door made him jump. He walked to the door and opened it to find his workmate, Jim Brewer, moving past the doorway and into Betts's apartment.

"Hey man!" said Brewer in a boisterous friendly tone. "You left work early and I was checking in on you. Are you sick? Is everything okay?"

James Alexander Brewer was a former master trooper with the Virginia State Police. He had gotten a clearance to work on the JTTF in the FBI Washington Field Office, and the lure of better money and field operations compelled him to apply for a CIA staff position. At thirty-four years of age with several years as an army warrant officer and four years on the FBI's Washington Field Office – Joint Terrorism Task Force (WFO/JTTF), he had been admitted to the *short course*, which provided much of the critical training for case officers in a much quicker time frame than the one-year operations training cycle that had produced top-quality intelligence officers since 1947. The accelerated course recognized experience from previous endeavors, and Brewer and Betts found themselves next to each other (the classes were seated in alphabetical order) for weeks of training that led to them working together at the agency's name-trace office in Vint Hill Farms.

"I'm fine. I got an offer to work overseas and lost my girlfriend in the process," Betts said flatly. The empty glass in his hand and the half empty bourbon bottle on the kitchen counter told Brewer all he needed to know.

"Well, I never met her, so I can't commiserate," Brewer said as he pushed past Betts and headed into the kitchen. Brewer had been here several times before, and he knew where everything was laid out.

"But I'll drink with you to celebrate! I got an assignment as well!"

Brewer's infectious positivity perked Betts up a bit.

"Really?" Betts said, turning to follow him into the kitchen.

Brewer went on an elongated speech as he fished in the cabinet for another glass, drew two cubes of ice from the freezer and poured himself two generous fingers of the famous Kentucky bourbon with the distinctive jewel-shaped bottle and race-horse cap.

"You are headed to Bosnia to conduct interviews of displaced Muslims who have survived being massacred by the Serbs in Srebrenica, while I have been asked to go to Islamabad, Pakistan to fill in for liaison operations. The analyst who was working with the Paks had to come home early in a two-year post, so they need someone, anyone, to cover the account! That's me, brother!"

"That's really great news!" said Betts as he clinked his glass with Brewer. "When do you leave?"

"I'm scheduled for shots and briefings at HQ first of next week. So I'm heading out earlier than you. Sorry to abandon you Randy, but this is a real chance!" Brewer said after a good swallow and loud throat-clearing.

"Are you going to run across the Potomac River and kiss your FBI guys goodbye?"

The FBI Washington Field Office, the second-largest field office in the US, was situated on Buzzard's Point near the WDC waterfront and FBI HQ. Each office housing a Joint Terrorism Task Force was FBI property, and the various agencies attending the JTTF were constantly reminded. As a cleared representative of the Virginia State Police, Brewer had made some great relationships with the Bureau agents working the counterterrorism (CT) account, along with DEA, BATFE, WDC Metropolitan Police, CIA, and Immigration Service agents in the task force, and they worked seamlessly to investigate any terrorist threat in Northern Virginia and Washington, DC. The WFO/JTTF tried to work assets and operations in neighboring Maryland, but the Baltimore JTTF (FBI/BFO/JTTF) jealously guarded their territory.

"Those guys kissed me goodbye the second I took a job with the agency," Brewer admitted. "They have very little love for spooks. The agency guys that work the JTTF are considered outsiders by both sides. FBI thinks they're spying on them, and CIA thinks they're beholden to two masters."

"Well, here's hoping your work in Pakistan is better received," Betts said as he clinked his glass again with Brewer.

"Thanks man. Randy, I'm really gonna miss you. Stay safe out there, and bring back some terrorist scalps," Brewer said soberly.

He was on the WFO/JTTF in February of 1993 when the World Trade Center garage under the North Tower was blown up by a van loaded with almost a ton of low-explosives, killing seven and wounding about a thousand people. The terrorist's plan was to make the North Tower collapse into the South Tower, which would kill tens of thousands of people. What prevented that was the poor placement of the van and the rigidity of the support structures in the garage. Brewer knew full well that those who planned this attack were animals, and all they deserved was the justice of lethal injection. The only choice was whether that injection was from a needle full of heart-stopping chemicals or the insertion of a jacketed hollow-point round from a 9-mm handgun. Brewer didn't care which.

"I'll miss you too," Betts said as his mood improved slightly. He was going to miss Jim Brewer, a former cop with a straightforward manner and deep-seated devotion to protecting his country.

The two men continued to finish the bottle together, making promises to remain in touch and exchanged office numbers for their respective CIA open lines. As cell phones and the calling plans for them were not cheap, neither had purchased one for personal use yet but would provide them when they did.

Chapter Seven

14 January 1996
Matha Toreed Bakery, Bihać, Bosnia-Herzegovina

The force of sound waves can create varying effects on a person. The lyrical mastery of string instruments in a well-conducted orchestra can result in soothing emotions and feelings of inclusion. The wave of sound and air blasts from an explosion can result in immediate anxiety and a physical response. Even when the explosion is not close—several city blocks away—the blast can create a percussion wave that can be as deadly as the heat and cutting force of being nearby.

Munir felt this blast wave come across him and the others, and the resulting movement of the concrete building and the screams it created made for a nauseating feeling in his stomach. He was unsure how much more they could stand of this.

Munir, Hamid, and roughly two dozen others were huddled into the rear storage room of a local bakery. The rigid old building was the last refuge they could find in this hellhole of a town. The Muslims in this enclave, who had lived here for generations in peace, had been herded into this portion of the town by heavily armed Serbs and told that this *United Nations safe zone* would keep them out of the fight with their aggressive neighbors to the East, the Croats.

According to the Serb militia commanders, the Croats were blindly firing West across the Danube River at these towns, that the true enemy was Croatia, and the only way to stop them was to fire back when the Muslim neighborhoods were safely moved further to the South. But before they were transported to this *safe zone*, the Serbs had relieved them of their weapons. For public safety, they were told. The late arrival of Munir and Hamid with loaded AK-47s that had been smuggled with them made the two boys something of a messiah to the small crowd of survivors. Maybe now the Muslims could plan to stage a revolt against the Serbs and retake their homes.

But now it was clear that this plan was not working, as the Serb artillery shells were falling on them and killing dozens every day. The "valiant fight against the Christian crusaders" described by his instructors in Pakistan was a struggle to survive in a live-fire zone where lulls in the artillery shelling allowed Serb snipers to pick off survivors as they tried to gather food and medical attention. This was the evilest display of warfare Munir could imagine, and upon arriving in the northern city of Cruzin, he quickly abandoned any idea of fighting back and undertook to scavenge food and supplies for anyone. Nearly all of the other young men who had traveled this dangerous route to come to the aid of Muslims were dead. The artillery barrages and merciless sniping had whittled this *valiant fight* down to the two confused boys from Chitral. Munir's efforts to escape the shelling moved him, Hamid, and this group south to Bihać, where he found this bakery, formerly owned by an elderly couple who served up hot bread and rolls at 5:00 a.m. every morning.

They had been killed early in the fighting here, as 7.62-caliber coaxial machine guns from Serbian M-84 tanks tore through the town and undertook Operation Tiger. This military operation, designed to wipe out the Bosnian Muslim population, resulted in residents sandbagging their homes and begging local politicians for help.

None had come in the last three years, and Munir was now certain that his effort to keep this small group alive meant that he would have to move from here. The force of the blast convinced him that the shelling was starting back up and getting closer now that the Serbs knew where they were hiding. In this back room, The power was out, and no windows could allow light in, so everyone had been suffering together in the dark for over two days. The food was gone, the injuries were unattended, and the lack of hygiene was stifling. The shelling had subsided slightly, but now this blast...

Several minutes after the last explosion, Munir was getting his hearing back, and he thought about taking down the heavy steel racks that they had piled against the front door of this room. That door led to the office and bathroom area and beyond to the bakery sales floor. The only other exit to this dark room was the back door, which led to the loading dock. This back entrance consisted of two heavy wooden doors bolted securely to the stone wall. Evidently, the old couple had not wished for anyone to break into the back of their bakery.

But Munir knew that going out by that door was suicide; the loading dock had no cover, and the residential buildings surrounding the block where the bakery was built allowed any sniper an easy view of anyone exiting the back door. No, it had to be the door leading to the front.

And then the back door was broken open from the outside.

The twin heavy wooden doors cracked, splintered, and suddenly flew backward. They collapsed with a controlled, hard crunch that sounded like some dinosaur had simply bitten them off the building.

But no dinosaurs still existed, so Munir and the others were simply stunned into staring at the bright light of day flooding the room and the dissipating dust from the hinges that had given up so easily. There was no fight left in them; this was the end.

"G'day mate! Is all a' you aw-right?" was the booming call from the doorway. Munir spoke several languages, but this shouting was nothing he had ever heard before. Some of it sounded like English, but some of it sounded…foreign.

"Can't beyin theyah if yoo gotta gun," came the next perplexing shout. Munir took a slight step forward.

"Yoo ahm'd?" Munir heard something about the tone. He couldn't understand the language, but the tone of the voice shouting appeared to be patient, nonthreatening.

Munir stepped closer to the doorway, and he could see the heavy doors lying on the ground twenty feet from the loading dock; they had been chained to the back of a large military truck that had simply driven forward and yanked the doors off their hinges. This is how they had been pulled out so cleanly. Then he heard that strange voice again.

"I say agin. Due yoo have any weapons in theyah?" Now Munir understood, they wanted any guns the group held.

Munir called to Hamid and had him bring the two Kalashnikov rifles they had been issued when they first arrived. These were clean and loaded but never fired. He held them over his head, high in his hands, and he walked slowly out the back door. The others in the group were cowering in fear and dread, and they begged him in both Bosnian and Arabic not to trust these invaders. Munir knew that they had no choice. This hiding was over.

An infantry soldier in full military gear quickly and quietly stepped up to him from around the corner of the doorway, took the rifles from his hands and handed them off to another soldier that had advanced on his left. This soldier turned away with the two rifles and spoke quickly into a lapel microphone.

"G'day to you mate!" said the initial soldier in a much quieter, softer tone. "Sorry for the delay, but we couldn't rush in on you and get shot now, could we?"

Munir blinked hard, and finally asked, "What language do you speak? Are you Bosnian?" The words sounded like English, but he could not decipher the message.

"Nah, I'm Crowat! Top Kick Krucic at your service! My accent is a bit Aussie, 'cause I grew up near Brisbane! But when the Woor stahted, came home to muy native land, y'know?"

Munir processed this quickly and understood his situation; they were being rescued by the Croation army.

"I am Munir, sir," he said quickly. "We have over twenty people in here; many of them need food and medical attention. Can I..."

The sergeant turned so quickly it alarmed Munir. The heavy equipment and weapons the sergeant carried seemed to be weight-less, as he waved his arms and motioned to the line of similarly equipped soldiers standing a dozen meters away.

"Surveyvers heyah! Get me stretchahs and the doc right now!"

Munir looked over to see the second soldier that had approached, bending down and stripping the AK-47s with a speed that his instructors had never displayed. Once the rifles were clear, the soldier gathered the disabled rifles under one arm and held the magazines in the other hand as he hustled off to a pile of other rifles gathered in the street.

"Thank you for coming, for your help," was the only thing he could summon.

The weeks of running, hiding, searching and doing anything to stay alive had been an incredible strain on him. This last week with these Bosnians, trying to understand their story and their injuries and allay their fears had been a mighty weight on Munir, and it was finally lifting. He covered his face with his hands. The relief was too much right now.

"You're okay now, mate," said Krucic as he placed his hand on Munir's shoulder.

"Don't you worry a bit. Doc's gonna fix up your crew; we'll get ya fed and bedded in no time. Not to worry. Furst, I'm gonna have you talk to my buddy, and he'll get everything sorted out!"

Top Sergeant Nethaniel "Neddie" Krucic of the Croatian army, 204th Vukovar Brigade, gently guided Munir from the loading dock to the sidewalk around to the front of the bakery. The streets were littered with crumbled rock and crumpled steel, body parts, burning vehicles and black patches of blast marks. Bihać, the administrative center of the Una Santa Canton of the Republic of Bosnia-Herzegovina, was a shambles of death, destruction, and desolation.

"Sorry for that last blast," explained Sergeant Krucic as he guided Munir across the street toward a huge white tent in front of a large stone building. "We had a T-55 that would not quit, and he finally had to be put down."

The sergeant motioned to his left as they walked, and Munir saw a burning hulk one hundred meters away that had been an old Soviet tank. It was burning fiercely, and the ammunition was cooking off as they approached the tent.

Munir and the sergeant bent slightly to enter the tent, whereupon Munir saw a jigsaw of folding tables arrayed at eight-foot lengths with medical equipment and supplies piled into almost every corner. A staff of over a dozen people with Red Cross armbands were looking over several locals, and Munir hoped that his group would come here next.

They walked through the emergency medical response center and stopped at the entrance to a tunnel of tentlike material that led to a door. This would have been the door leading into the three-story stone building behind the tent. When they stopped at the door, the sergeant's demeanor seemed to change. He turned to face Munir and said in a clear, quiet voice that demanded attention, "Now mate, I'm going to search you very quickly. Nothing to get prickled about; it's just routine."

He went over Munir's arms and legs very quickly and ran his hand over the canteen under Munir's shirt.

"Is that a weapon or explosive of some sort?" said Krucic warily.

"No sir, it's my canteen."

Upon bringing it out from his tunic, Krucic examined it and squeezed slightly.

"And it's a beauty at that! Did you find this local?" Krucic asked.

"No, my mother made it for me."

"Well Munir, your mum's a wondah," said Krucic earnestly. "The only thing my mum made me was skinny and dangerous!" he said, laughing loudly. Munir couldn't help but smile at this big, loud, earthy man with military prowess and a generous heart.

Krucic knocked and opened the door of the stone building at the same time and ushered Munir into a large conference room with one table, a desk, and two chairs. One of the chairs was empty. It sat across the table from the other chair, in which a man sat with an ink pen poised over a legal pad on the table.

"This one came out with all the guns. All he had on 'im was this canteen. He got medical and food for his group, about two dozen. You'll meet 'em when the docs are done!" The sergeant stated in a low, pleasant tone that resembled much better English. Evidently, this person had trouble with Krucic's Australian accent too.

The sergeant guided Munir to the sole empty chair, and once he sat down Krucic placed his hand on the shoulder of the other man. This was a civilian with a nonmilitary haircut and an even gaze. He looked at Munir with interest and a polite smile. Nothing threatening here. Not yet.

"Munir, my boy, meet Randall. He's gonna ask you some questions and get you all the help you need!"

With that, the sergeant walked quietly out of the room through the doorway he had entered with Munir. After the door was shut, he could hear Krucic's loud, commanding voice issuing instructions to his troops.

Munir now sat straight in his chair and tried to get a sense of this man; he studied Munir for a moment and finally said, "Hello, my name is Randall Betts. Where are you from, Munir?"

Part Two

Chapter Eight

Later in the day, 14 January 1996
Reading room of the Dušan Grabrijan Library, Bihać, Bosnia

"So, what are you?" Munir said, finally starting to relax.

After almost two hours of introductions and questions about how he arrived in Bihać, he had tired of the onslaught of curiosity from this American. Munir had answered all the questions put to him about his home, his family heritage, and his reasons for undertaking this effort. Munir was open about the routes and transits and movements he had made to get here; he had nothing to hide. Munir concluded that his interrogator was an American because of his very simple questions and his ignorance of the geography. Munir had to show him three times the route he and Hamid had taken from the Khyber Pass to the various points they had stowed away in until they arrived in Rijeka.

"Well, let's just say I'm the guy who's going to get you out of this mess," replied Betts.

After an extensive vetting of this young man through open-ended questions and false recapping, he was glad that Munir had asked him a question. It would (hopefully) demonstrate a desire to continue talking. Munir's story and background were amazing, the fact that he and his brother had gotten this far after all the unsafe traveling and intense fighting was proof that this young man had all the moxie he needed.

"How? By throwing us into your prison? Handing us over to the Serbs?" Munir strained to show some indignation with this question, even though it sounded like it came from a frightened child.

"Those are not the options available to me," answered Betts with honesty.

"Well, what is it you want?" Munir adopted a visage of impatience as he counted on his fingers. "You've learned all you can about me, about Hamid. So what else can I tell you? We haven't hurt anyone, we haven't infected anyone with our Islamic faith, we haven't..."

Betts cut him off with a simple statement.

"We are going to arrange for safe travel for you and your brother out of the country. The US State Department will have both of you listed as refugees and resettle you back home, if that's what you want. But based on what you've told me, I think you may ask for some other landing point."

Munir eyed Betts now with a look of skepticism.

"And why would I do that? My home is Chitral in the frontier province of Pakistan."

"But you and Hamid were hoping to travel and see the world," Betts replied and waved his hand over the city behind them. "But this isn't exactly the world you were seeking. And all the other places you've been consisted of huddling in the cargo hold of a ship or curled up under a blanket in back of a truck."

Betts had taken extensive notes from Munir's travels, and these notes would result in no fewer than a dozen disseminated intelligence cables on terrorist smuggling routes in East Asia and East Europe. The Counter Terrorist Center (CTC) would benefit greatly from this one interview. As he was a first-tour case officer, Betts should have been using an alias. But the aid organizations insisted that he use his true name.

Betts continued, "Where did your travel people say they would take you next?"

"They did not say," Munir said with a degree of honesty. He needed a chance to get away from here safely, and the American was not wrong; the last thing he and Hamid would want was being delivered back to Chitral, where his family would suspect and the ISID would come for him again. Not a good option.

Munir decided to try and play this out a bit.

"What they did say was something about camps in the mountains south of Russia for more training and education."

Betts ran down a quick list of options available: if Pakistan would be out for Munir, then where else? His management would not allow travel to any fancy European capital, and lots of smaller places, like Amsterdam or Vienna, would recoil at the thought of taking anyone known to have an association with a terrorist network. He thought quickly and came to the same conclusion that Munir had: Chechen camps in the Kist region of the Pankisi Gorge, Republic of Georgia.

Betts remembered a cable that was disseminated two weeks before he left Vint Hills Farm. The cable was from the Georgian capital of Tbilisi, and the local security service was asking the CIA station chief if he had any satellite imagery of the Kist Mountains in the northeastern part of Georgia. This area was exploited heavily by the Russians after a series of raids by Chechen separatists in the early 1990s, and their bombing and *counterterrorist raids* into Northern Georgia had turned up nothing. The cable surmised that the Georgians were aware of the Chechens preserving their camps in this region but couldn't find them. They wanted the US to help find them.

"Tell you what," Betts began as he spread a map of East Europe over the table in front of Munir. "If I can get you to the bridge that links Armenia and Georgia and buy you the gear and clothing for long-distance hiking, could you make it into those areas in Northern Georgia?"

"Buy us nothing," Munir said quietly. "Get us to Armenia without making us bend low in a barrel and give me the funds to buy the things we need, and Hamid and I will be there in two weeks."

Betts was shocked at this young man. He was really made of stern stuff to make an offer such as this, and Betts was willing to take the chance. This would be a minimal effort to transport Munir and Hamid to Armenia; all they would need would be some basic travel documents. These would take less than a week to process out of the State Department, as they would be eager to establish these boys' identities no matter where they were going. From there, Betts would take funds from his operational account and exchange it from US dollars to Georgian lari. That would give the two brothers plenty of money for food, clothing, backpacking gear, and anything else to get them on this journey. This could be done. And it could be done clandestinely with the help of Munir.

"Look, I'm not talking about how quickly you can get there. Just that you get there safely without raising the suspicions of the people you work for."

"We don't work for them," answered Munir suddenly. "We were fooled into this adventure, and they are dedicated to a war against the West that I don't understand. I've been told extravagant things about how evil and dangerous Americans and Europeans are, and how they are trying to wipe out the Islamic faith. I'm not Muslim, strictly speaking, but I come from an Islamic nation, and although they treat us like lepers, I'm not going to sit in Chitral District and just let the West run over us!"

"I'm certain you've figured this out for yourself Munir, but they have lied to you," Betts said quietly, putting his hands on the table and trying to lay out his position without seeming to be parochial or smarmy. Munir had demonstrated intelligence and a genuine desire to be honest with him, and Betts had a chance here to see if that honesty was fake or simply an effort to draw out a CIA officer for capture. This would be dicey;

"Munir, your faith is not why I make this offer to you, and the challenge that the Kalash face back home is exactly what I want you to consider. The government doesn't hold your people in high esteem because Islam is the official religion of Pakistan. That lack of tolerance is nothing we can conquer in one lifetime, but working with me we can show to the Pakistani government that religious freedom is a preferable stance by highlighting the effort to rid the world of Islamic extremists that wage war against all nonbelievers."

Munir was lost a bit on this. "So how does this hiking trip solve anything?"

Betts was ecstatic at this point. Munir was holding him to the present tense, to the real-world offer for him and Hamid. It helped him understand that Munir wasn't trying to play games or engage in hyperbole.

He leaned forward in his chair and replied, "Your willingness to take this trip and safely stay in the fold of these people, these extremists, will help us better identify and avoid the threat they pose to innocent people everywhere."

"And what then? Just give them up to you? Didn't your own people blow up their government building?" Munir raised. He needed to believe in this American, but many points and views had been made to him in the past few weeks.

Betts spoke quickly.

"You're not giving up anybody. We need to learn more about their plans and actions that threaten innocent people. And yeah, American radicals killed a lot of Americans last year, more than the Hezbollah extremists in Lebanon, but I'll tell you this: if we had known that these evil assholes were planning that attack in Oklahoma, we'd have been more interested in stopping the bombing, not just jailing and killing people for thinking about it."

Munir was more than relieved to hear this. Betts was showing that he had the right path, and that he could get him and his brother out of this crappy situation with very little strings. Wait, he thought, what strings?

"And what do I owe you for this? Be your reporter? Be your whore to report on the men who sleep with me?" Munir's father taught him to show some grit when you are digging in the dirt.

"Munir, you don't owe me for this. If anything, these people owe you. You have proven yourself to be resourceful and dedicated to the mission they have laid before you. What I'm proposing is that when you get back in the camps with these folks, you lay low and continue with the training they provide. After some time, I'm going to travel through the region by car and I hope to be able to meet with you privately."

Betts was thinking on his feet as he played this out, but he was unsure if Munir would take all this on board.

"And how will you find me?" Munir asked.

"With this."

Betts reached across the table and picked up the distinctive canteen his mother made.

"You put this in a prominent place near where you're staying, between lunch and dinner time. I'll recognize the canteen and drive just down the road and wait. When you can get away, like taking a walk after dinner, come and find me, and we'll talk."

"Talk about what?" Munir was getting to the dirt now. This American had an agenda, and he could be trying to get Munir and Hamid in a trap that could threaten them further.

"If you have learned anything that could be useful, great. If nothing has come up yet, fine. I'm not willing to risk you or your brother's safety. It's important to me that we survive this, and if you have to travel out before I get there, or if you have something that you think is really important, use this."

With this, Betts pulled the cheapest cell phone he could buy in Bosnia and handed it to Munir. He had not brought this out until he was certain that Munir could pull this off.

"I'm going to give you an emergency number and an unusual word that only you and I understand. If you call my number and use that word in a sentence, I'll know it's you, and you're safe. But if you or anyone else calls my number and doesn't use that word, then I'll know that you have been threatened by these thugs. And I will do all that I can to save you."

"What's the word?" asked Munir slyly. He was getting the idea here, and he felt he had one of two things: No choice or nothing to lose. At this point, working with this American was his only option.

"How about Krucic?" Betts folded his hands in front of him, hopeful that Munir would understand.

"The sergeant? You want to use his name?" Munir asked, smiling now.

"Neddy is a great guy. He has been an enormous help in coordinating my work while arranging for Red Cross operations and Operation Storm. It isn't easy to satisfy multiple masters, but Sergeant Krucic has been nothing less than stellar in taking care of the Bosnians who have endured so much while inflicting punishment on the Serbs who tried to wipe them out."

"I've never met anyone like him," Munir said in a grateful tone. "Why Armenia?" He said, changing the subject quickly. Munir was thinking this offer over and was thinking about how he would propose this to Hamid, who was probably in the medical tent with the others by now.

"The Armenians are in the middle of an undeclared war, and they process lots of refugees for travel to Georgia. They think of it as passing off their problems to their unhelpful neighbor. Anyway, it'll work. I'll get you some updated Pak passports while you and Hamid rest up. Take this document to the Red Cross in the tent outside, and they'll direct you to where you start processing."

Betts slid a paper out of his yellow pad and furiously filled in some of the lines on it.

Chapter Nine

Two days later, 16 January 1996
Hotel Bled, Ljubljana, Slovenia

"I don't want to hear another word. Pack your bags and call the airline to change your ticket. I'm getting you out of my country right now!"

The rushed words came from the mouth of the CIA Station Chief in one of the finest hotels in the capital. The stress in his voice made the sentence sound like he was being strangled as he spoke them.

Hotel Bled was a grand old granite structure that had housed many of the visitors to former President Tito's vacation villas during the time that Yugoslavia was a complete nation. Now that Yugoslavia had broken into several smaller countries (and some of them continued to be at war with each other), the newly formed country of Slovenia was the hub of Bosnian war relief efforts. Hotel Bled had survived any conflict in the breakup, as it overlooked one of the finest large lakes in Europe and was home to the annual international rowing championship. With the embassy in Belgrade gone and the smaller CIA installations unable to handle the enormous amount of ops traffic coming out of the war zone, Ljubljana was chosen as the central point of coordination for the CIA efforts in Bosnia.

"Chief, I'm telling you that this kid has the tools and the brains for this," insisted Betts as he leaned in toward the COS as they had lunch on the outside café overlooking the large, tranquil lake.

"Since when do you get to make these decisions? This is not some military fly-by-night operation where you have to do or die. You have a chain of command and a very simple mission: interview these people, get them logged into the system, and flag the dangerous ones; don't make some halfhearted recruitment and hand over taxpayer dollars to get them backpacking into Georgia! Did you at least clear this with Tbilisi Station?"

COS Ljubljana was in his midthirties with a decent suit and blond hair that needed a haircut. His fierce rejection of Betts's idea of sending Munir and Hamid into territory near Chechnya was immediate, and his temper was just below the surface. Betts knew that this was a *turf* issue—that you couldn't just waltz an unproven asset into somebody's area of responsibility and not coordinate. Betts was ready this time; he had done some homework.

"CTC has approved the idea, and they have obligated the funds to get them..." Betts couldn't finish trying to calm the COS down.

"They don't own this turf! They can obligate all the money they want, but it is the local station that approves the op!" He was leaning forward, trying to make his point without raising his voice loud enough to be heard in the outdoor café.

"I'm trying to tell you, that's being done right now," Betts answered quietly.

"Who is getting this done? I've heard nothing about this, and you sure as hell have not sent any cables through me!"

"That's why I asked you to meet me. I need to get into your

station and write this up; HQ wants this to be documented as soon as possible."

"Why would I do the bidding of the Counter-Terrorist Center (CTC)?"

"It's not just for CTC. It's for the White House." Betts let that sink in a bit.

"What are you talking about? How is the White House involved in this small-minded idea?" The COS was surprised at this, but he was being stubborn.

Betts said, "the State Department called the White House to throw a fit about Russia planning another excursion into Georgia if something isn't done about the Chechen separatists moving back and forth across the border after raiding Russian supply depots near Dagestan. So the president pulled in the Russian Ambassador and told him that the US would work with Georgia to clean out Chechen camps in the Kist territory North of Tbilisi. The White House called the director of central intelligence and demanded reporting about the size and locations of these Chechen camps. Munir and Hamid are perfect to keep us apprised of this."

The *court intrigue* of this explanation had the COS Ljubljana twisting in his chair while he listened. This was something almost as big as the war in Bosnia. This was something that could further enhance his importance to the DCI.

"Okay," said the COS. "I'm going to open up the office, and you're going to write this plan up. You're going to make HQ know that we came up with this idea and that you are going to keep me apprised of their progress."

Betts looked at him, listening, waiting for the rest of his statement. It came.

"And then you're going to call the airline and change your ticket to Georgia and get the hell out of my territory."

Betts was somewhat surprised at this. What the COS was *rec-*

ommending was to seek coordination and concurrence with Tbilisi Station to allow him to go to Georgia and handle Munir and Hamid directly. This was actually a welcome turn of events for Betts; he could get out of this boring routine of interviewing Islamic refugees in Bihać and actually run an operation in the field. He could finish travel arrangements for Munir and Hamid, then fly to Tbilisi, getting to the capitol way before two guys backpacking from Armenia, and try to find a way to stay in touch with Munir. This was sounding better all the time.

"Well, you're the boss," Betts said as he stood from the patio table and followed COS Ljubljana out of the hotel. As they passed through the lobby of the hotel, Betts looked over to see the expansive bank of pay phones along the wall, and reminded himself to call Denise when he got to a phone in the Embassy. Calling from overseas was way too expensive, and he wanted to hear her voice again. Even if she only had venom for what he was doing, he wanted to hear her again.

As Betts was preparing his cable to CTC and Tbilisi Station (with additional concurrence requested from Yerevan) laying out this backpacking operation, Munir and Hamid were standing in line outside of a Red Cross center just outside of Cazin. The people here, efficient and civil, were too busy to pay attention to anyone in particular. Refugees would come off the bus from Bihać, be hustled into a medical tent for a check-up (and bandages if needed), then have their papers rifled through before being segregated into travel centers. Munir had seen this kind of operation before when he visited a meat-processing center in Karachi and saw how the cattle were treated.

But overall they were being fed and cared for, and they were in line to get travel documents which would allow them to travel safely through Europe or to their home country. The American Betts had set up the two for travel to Yerevan, Armenia as Muslim refugees. It would get them into Armenia, but not across the border into Georgia.

That part of the trip would entail an illegal crossing, and Betts had given them maps and some suggestions of areas where the border guard service was not as vigilant. Some risk was involved, but overall, Munir's anxiety was one of anticipation, not dread. This was the best way to truly see the world. The Caucuses region was supposed to be beautiful, and getting there was a challenge where Munir and Hamid were in charge, not some bilious smuggler intent on getting paid and uncaring about those in his charge. Munir hoped they were out of that tragic game forever.

"Do you think they'll fire on us when we get to Armenia?" asked Hamid as he studied the Polaroid picture of him and his Kalash family once more.

"Not unless we're Iranians," said Munir with a smirk. "They may dislike Sunni Muslim refugees in their country, but they hate the Shia even more."

"It'll be nice to get to travel without hiding," Hamid said as he tucked the picture neatly back into his canteen skin.

"Oh, we're traveling like kings," crowed Munir. "They're flying us to Armenia on a big airplane!"

"Really? Is it that far?" Hamid was standing a bit straighter now. "Over 1,700 miles."

Munir had studied the maps the American Betts had provided and knew the airport out of Bosnia was not a big one. They would be using smaller planes to get there, but that was going to be part of the adventure. Munir was regaling Hamid with all the places and people they'd be visiting just as they were hurriedly brought into the travel office for their documents and ticketing.

Chapter Ten

Three Weeks Later, Early February 1996
Tbilisi, Georgia

"It feels good to be out of the city," Bondarenko Georgadze said as he maneuvered the Toyota SUV through the curves of the mountainous Saguramo Range. They were traveling at four thousand feet above sea level, and while the mountains were beautiful, "Bondo" was driving too fast on these gravel roads.

"We've been out of the city for two days! But we might not make it back if we crash out here!" Betts said in a pleasant but frightened tone.

"You're just not used to the mountains. Everything is fine; don't you worry," Bondo said as he switched back to the other side of the road to hustle through another blind curve.

Betts and Bondo were joined together by the chiefs of both Tbilisi Station and the Georgian Border Guard Service. This was the first time the two services had worked together, and it only got off the ground after the US president made a polite call to the Georgian president and asked for his assistance in keeping the Russians from invading Georgia again.

The Russians invaded Georgia in 1992 after the breakup of the Soviet Union. They assumed a large portion of Northwest Georgia in the Abkhazia region and created a huge problem for Georgian refugees fleeing the area. As Georgia was not keen to allow the same thing to happen in the northeastern part of the country (two hundred miles north of the capital), they quickly arranged for Bondo and an official vehicle to escort Betts into the mountains to look over the issue of Chechen separatists camping in the woods just over the Russian border.

The mountains here were breathtaking. Betts had grown up around foothills of pine and oak-wooded parts of Tennessee, but the bluffs and lakes and castles of this region, a protected area known as the Tbilisi National Park, was too gorgeous to describe. Even with all the pristine beauty, Betts knew there was danger here.

They were heading to the Pankisi Gorge, a region of Kist people who tolerated the Chechen rebels from Dagestan because they hated the Russians. The uneasy coexistence was a delicate balance, and the interference of any outsiders made these small villages that spread throughout the woods a haven of mistrust and suspicion.

Bondo Georgadze was an experienced border guard agent. His badge and his CZ-75 9-mm pistol got him into any part of the border region that he desired, but he knew this area was more bandit country politics than illegal immigrant problems. That said, Bondo was a proud Georgian, and he knew that the Kist people hated the Russians as much as he did. Having some measure of acceptance could be attained through a genuine desire to help and a healthy show of government power. Bondo had been instructed to gather information about how many Chechens were living among the Kist villages and try to sow some distrust of the Dagestani Muslims if he could.

After several hours of driving from the old capitol Mtskheta (where they had stayed the night due to Bondo's lack of sobriety), Betts and Bondo found themselves driving behind an old Moskva sedan and entering a small village area that included some tents, shacks, and what appeared to be a shed for smoking meat. It was a very rural village, but there were several people walking about, so it had a pretty good-sized population. Betts looked intently to see if anyone was staring at the dark blue SUV with Georgian government tags that they were riding in, but he could not discern any *stink eye*.

And then he saw it. A small colorful canteen was hanging outside the window of one of the shacks. This was Munir's signal. He and

Hamid were here with those who had sent him to Bosnia, hopefully the terrorists he was looking for.

"Bondo! This is the place. Pull over just outside the village!" Betts said with a voice of sudden excitement.

"But this is just some shit camp! We are fifty miles from the border!" said Bondo.

"Yeah, I know. But I have a hunch that what we are looking for can be here," Betts said in a slightly calmer voice. The presence and participation of Munir had been kept secret from the Georgians. Not strictly due to lack of trust, but for the protection of Munir as a potential reporter for CIA. Betts had been careful to segregate his knowledge of Munir's travels (especially his illegal incursion from Armenia into Georgia) from the Border Guard Service. If Munir would be arrested, Betts could arrange for a quiet release and hustle him out of the country, but if he was able to reintegrate himself and Hamid into this group, the information could be critical to CTC.

Just then Bondo quietly said, "What the fuck is this?"

Betts turned from his lock on the colorful Kalash canteen on the right-hand side of their SUV to the windshield. What he suddenly saw was the start of something unearthly. As the beat-up old Moskva sedan in front of them negotiated a sharp turn in the muddy dirt road passing through this village, two sets of two armed men advanced on both sides of the car and motioned for it to stop. As the weathered sedan eased and squeaked to a stop, the four men raised their SKS rifles at the car and screamed some demands in a language neither man recognized. The two men on the driver's side raised their aim from the rifle's stock to shout orders at the terrified occupants of the sedan, while the two men on the passenger's side kept their armed gaze locked onto the car.

Bondo had slowed, but not stopped. He was slowly advancing on the scene from about twenty-five meters and drew his badge from his left coat pocket and then switched hands and drew his pistol from the holster on his right hip.

And then everything exploded. The four men on cue opened up on the Moskva sedan, starting with the hood area and slowly raked fire into the windshield and passenger compartment, sending smoke and shards of metal and glass into the air.

"Backup, BACKUP!" Betts shouted as he too drew the Glock Model 19 pistol issued to him at the station. Bondo fiddled for a moment, and when he saw the attention of the four men shift from the bullet-riddled smoking sedan blocking the roadway to that of the government SUV approaching, he quickly put the vehicle into reverse and commanded it to scream backward.

Bondo's whip of the steering wheel created a skid and spin back into the direction in which they had come. That's when the unrelenting crack of sonic 7.62 x 39 millimeter bullets and the frightening crunch of sheet metal being hit by gunfire started. Betts's passenger side window cracked into a full view of irregular glass shards, so he pushed the broken window out and reached out with his left hand to return fire at the men. After his second round was fired, he heard Bondo draw a sharp breath and looked to see his driver grabbing the side of his bloodied head.

Two rounds had come through the back window and exited out the windshield. One of the two rounds clipped the rim of Bondo's right ear, and while the injury was not critical, it stunned him and bled well. He was clutching the ear with the pistol in his right hand while his left hand was trying to hold the steering wheel. Betts quickly reached up and eased the bloody pistol from Bondo's grip and assessed the wound. It had taken off a good chunk of his ear, but the bullet had not grazed the skull.

By the time Betts was grabbing into the medical kit in the back seat (covered up by clothing, bags, and water bottles), the shooting had stopped. Bondo was flying madly down the road from the village and putting good distance between them and the attackers. Betts came up with a triangular bandage first, and he ripped it from its bag and put it to Bondo's ear. This was not the intended use of this large triangular-shaped hunk of cloth, but it would do until they could stop safely and wrap the wound.

"You're okay Bondo. The bullet hit your ear, but it's just a lot of blood. You'll be fine," Betts finally said as he held the cloth material against the driver's head.

"Where's my gun?" was the first thing Bondo said, followed by a flurry of questions. "What the fuck happened back there? Who was that doing the shooting? Where are we now? Can you call my headquarters and tell them what happened? Why am I still bleeding? Are you hurt?"

Betts could not answer them quickly enough.

"We're fine Bondo. Pull us up inside this barn coming up."

Bondo looked confused through the broken windshield in front of him. He saw a large material storage shed up ahead on the right. He still wasn't thinking about anything but the thugs and murderers who just shot up his government-owned Toyota Highlander. This was an expensive vehicle, and his superiors were gonna be pissed about this.

"Why do we stop at the shed?" Bondo asked.

"You're going to drop me off here." Betts replied. When the quizzical look didn't dissipate, he continued.

"Look, you can't bring this car back down to your HQ with me in it and full of holes. It's best if nobody sees me with you, and people will notice the holes in this thing!"

As Bondo slowed up but prepared to ask the next question, Betts said, "You will go straight to your supervisor. He knew about us coming up here today. Tell him what happened, and before you get that ear looked at, send somebody up here to get me!"

"I will come back for you myself! And I'll bring the Georgian army with me. But we can't get back up here until well after dark!"

The car was now stopped next to the large shed. Betts had noticed it when they had approached the village. The shed was about two kilometers from the village, and Betts noticed when they drove by earlier that one door was affixed tightly to the frame but the other door hung open.

"No worries, my friend," he said as he opened the SUV door and swung out to dig into the back seat. "I've got a change of clothes, some water, and a medical kit. I'm all set."

Bondo kept looking worriedly at his new friend. He didn't like the idea of leaving this American in the woods, but his ear hurt like hell, and he wanted to get back down to the capitol.

"Oh yeah," Betts said, patting his waistline. "I have my pistol."

"Then you need this," Bondo said, as he stripped a fresh magazine from its holder on his waist and threw it to Betts. The magazine wouldn't fit the pistol, he knew, but the 9-mm hollow-point ammunition would.

"Thank you, partner. Don't come back yourself. Get somebody to stitch that ear. Send somebody from the US Embassy for me. They'll hustle up here, I know."

Bondo drove off, and Betts began to feel the woods and the cold and the afternoon chill. He searched through the medical kit and found a flashlight. Well, it looked like a flashlight. It was actually for checking a patient's ears for wax, so the beam was anything but bright. Betts swore he'd never travel out without a good light again.

As he was mentally building the materials for an appropriate bugout bag, Betts heard footsteps on the dirt road. They were moving at an appropriate pace, not running, and not creeping. Whoever it was, it was someone who belonged here. Betts didn't, so he drew his Glock 19 and stood inside the shed doors.

"Are you hiding in there mate?" came a voice that Betts recognized instantly. "Did you bring Sergeant Crew-sick with you?"

"It's pronounced K-R-O-O-S-H-I-C-S!" Betts said as he turned the corner of the door and shook Munir's hand with his right. He still held the Glock in his left hand.

"Did you come alone?" he asked, looking carefully beyond the shed toward the road.

"I'm alone. Hamid is back at the village. Are you okay?" said Munir quickly. He had heard the shots and stepped out just in time to see Betts shooting out from the passenger's side of the SUV as they sped away.

"I'm good. The other guy has gone back for help. What the hell was all that?"

Munir took a quick breath and started, "They are all worked up because a senior leader in the network is here. He's laying out a plan for bombing several embassies at once, and he needs a lot of timing and coordination. Everyone is all excited about blowing up Americans, and then a car with soldiers rolled through followed by border guards!"

Betts had to stop him as Munir was spouting both operational information and actionable intelligence all at the same time.

"Slow down buddy! Start at the beginning! What's this about embassies? Are they US embassies?"

Munir laid out a vivid but complex explanation about how the terrorist network, a heretofore unknown group known as Al-Qaeda formed under a Saudi sheikh who had declared a fatwa (holy war) against America last year. Al-Qaeda had devised a plan to attack US embassies all along the east coast of Africa. This was to be done in retaliation for the brazen invasion of Somalia. (The first fatality in Operation Restore Hope to bring food and stability to war-torn Somalia had been a marine corporal from third battalion, a Parris Island classmate of Betts's.)

As Betts tried to absorb all the information and recap to make sure he heard it right, he finally drew up and asked, "Wait, who's the senior leader that's here?"

"Hafez Al-Zedicki. He is a cruel, evil man who trusts no one, and he is wielding a lot of power and money through Al-Qaeda if anything he says is true."

Betts couldn't take it anymore. He had to fish into the med kit and retrieve a magic marker, then he pulled a dinner receipt from the restaurant he visited the night before.

"How do I spell that name?"

"Zed-ee-key!" said Munir quickly. "I have to get back! If anyone asks for me, it could get me in trouble if I'm not there!"

Betts was writing crib notes on the thin paper as Munir bolted back toward the village.

"Wait!" called Betts as quietly as he could. "Where can I catch you next?"

"All I know right now is that the first place they're targeting is Ethiopia! I'll be there in a few weeks!" called Munir in a whisper as he ran up the road.

"You mean the embassy in Ethiopia? Munir?" Betts called quietly again, but Munir was gone around a steep corner in the dirt road.

Back at the village, the last of the bodies and guns had been hauled out of the Moskva sedan that had been riddled with rifle fire earlier. The bodies were Russian soldiers, probably driving from one outpost to another. They posed no threat to the villagers, or the terrorists that had camped out here. They were simply in the wrong place at the wrong time, and they would not be missed. The gear and ammo had been removed, the bodies piled back into the rear seat, and the car rolled from the spot where it had been attacked and pushed over a nearby bluff. The sickening crunch of the car's body impacting the hillside after a ten-story fall guaranteed that the remains would never be found. It became part of the pile of trash and cast-off debris from the village.

At that moment, Hamid Afridi was standing at the back of a

large canvas tent, rigid and straight, as the AK-47 rifle was pointed at his midsection.

"So you are the one who brought these soldiers and government men to our camp!" said Hafez Al-Zedicki in a thin, tight voice.

As Hamid shook his head to indicate his denial, Al-Zedicki pointed to the colorful canteen strung around the Pashtun boy's neck.

"We saw this canteen hanging from your window, and the men in the government car recognized it, no?"

Just then Munir came into the tent where Al-Zedicki held a rifle in one hand and pointed with the other, both of them aimed at his adopted brother. Munir had snatched his canteen from his window after the shooting and stuffed it under his heavy coat as he snuck down the road to try and find the American.

"NO!" said Munir loudly. "He hasn't done anything! He is faithful to you!"

"Then he won't have anything to worry about when he visits with Allah." Al-Zedicki grabbed the wooden handguard with his left hand and opened fire with the AK-47, creating a lightning blast of sound and fury and blood and canvas as the back of the tent fell open and both halves of Hamid's body fell through it.

***

Six hours later, at 3:00 a.m., a one-ton Chevrolet pickup with US Embassy tags and United States Marine Corps printed on the door approached the shed. The truck's rear dual-axle tires eased through the icy mud, as the headlights bounced through the thick night mist. All four doors opened when the truck stopped, and both the first and second shift of the embassy guard force stepped out in full battle gear, M-16 A2 rifles at high ready.

Betts had met these guys and had drinks with them while he

was in Tbilisi awaiting the chance to ride up here. But now, in the cold early morning hour, in enemy territory, with the stories of shoot-outs and sudden violence, he was taking no chance of being a surprise. He couldn't remember all the words, but he knew he had to shout them.

"Betts, lance corporal Randall A! Marine security force regiment! Second fast company Yorktown!" was his call to these heavily armed people.

"Corporal, advance and be rushed the fuck out of here!" was the response.

Chapter Eleven

One year later, 11 June 1997
Addis Ketema area, Addis Ababa, Ethiopia

Randall Betts was tired. He had looked through this pair of binoculars one more time at the building across the street from the apartment rented by the Ethiopian National Intelligence and Security Service (NISS). The image was the same: sun-stained awnings covering a one-story TV repair service shop with numerous wires going into the roof. The image did not change, even though the people passing by were slightly dissimilar.

This assignment had gone on for months. Although listed as *temporary duty* to Addis Ababa for getting to the bottom of this threat, Betts had been living out of a tolerable rental house and working night and day with the local service. The sole breaks were infrequent visits to the local CIA station to keep his management apprised of the...nothing that was happening. But Betts didn't mind stopping in; it gave him a chance to call back to Denise in the US. Even with the time difference (3:00 p.m. in Ethiopia was 8:00 a.m. in the Northeast US), he tried to call as often as he could. Denise was happy to hear from Betts, for a time. Lately, she had had to keep the calls short due to some family matters, or she had not answered at all. This disappointing lack of communication and ineffective surveillance op was starting to wear on him.

Betts was staking out this repair shop, which was considered by the NISS to be a haven for foreign terrorists. The owner was a known hawala dealer, and an asset of the service testified under oath that Arabs came and went at this business. As Addis Ababa station had nothing else for Betts to do, he was assigned as the counter terrorism liaison with NISS. The service was capable and dedicated to rooting out foreign threats to the country, but they lacked coordination with the local and federal police and frequently were caught up in each other's webs. Between the differing agendas and scarce resources, the various services always seemed to be at each other's throats.

The apartment for this surveillance op, a bare two-bedroom space with no running water, was situated above a local restaurant. The restaurant owner owned the apartment, and shut off the upper-floor water supply so that his restaurant had sufficient flow. The smell of body odor, great food, and rotting garbage was almost too much for Betts, but he stayed with the surveillance op because he refused to give up on Munir.

In the year after their meeting in that cold, dark shed, Betts had championed the intelligence provided by Munir. Analysts grappled with the tangled arms that reached out beyond a simple camp in the Pankisi Gorge and provided reams of finished intelligence from the connections and answers provided by these two. And yet, more questions remained. Fat, happy overseers of the intelligence community, members of Congress who hadn't visited the region became overnight experts on the interacting connections between the counter-Russian Chechens and the blood-thirsty Islamic extremists who took tons of money from terrorist financiers and planned attacks with more and more precision.

The attack several months before on the military housing complex in Dharan, Saudi Arabia, killed nineteen Americans and wounded over five hundred. The use of a tanker truck carrying five thousand pounds of explosives collapsed the entire front of the Khobar Towers housing complex. This horrific result, along with the fact that the driver of the tanker truck jumped into a waiting vehicle just before the explosion, was a chilling replay of the attack on the Murrah building in Oklahoma City. The group allegedly responsible for the attack was an odd collection of Saudi and Lebanese citizens, and their funding was attributed to Al-Zedicki.

The terrorists were learning how to better use their assets and resources to inflict more destruction and death on the US. Betts felt that time was running out; that the threat was both real and building.

Munir was the one source who started this fiery interest. He was the one who exposed the link between the terrorist training camps in Waziristan and the smuggling routes throughout Southeast Asia. Munir's information about the compound where he trained was helping Islamabad Station identify support assets that would lead to further investigations. He provided the identity of Hafez Al-Zedicki to the intelligence analysts, and through his information of where and when Zedicki had surfaced, a great deal of targeting information about Al-Qaeda had been amassed. This was how it was supposed to work: the CIA, NSA, DIA, and FBI combined their resources to track and identify an enemy who had been inside the US in the recent past. Further records from INS and customs enforcement helped build a travel pattern that would be exploited; when Al-Zedicki tried to use these routes or stuck his head up the next time, the hunters would be ready.

All this from two meetings. Munir's identity was being closely guarded by the CIA, despite the frequent requests for more information. Congress and other federal agencies were turning up the heat on the Counter Terrorist Center to reveal how they were coming up with all this great information, but to no avail. CTC used every bit of what little power they had to stave off any congressional review, and the extensive layers of secrecy and nonattributable writing prevented Munir's name from ending up on the front page of the *Washington Post*. The chance of some staffer from one of the Select Intelligence Committees blabbing the name of Afridi to an ardent reporter was too great.

And something else happened. With the information from Munir and the confirmation of his information through analysis and previous threat reporting about Al-Qaeda, the USG was able to build a complete picture of this critical terrorist leader, Al-Zedicki, and his network. Confirmation from the White House and the state department resulted in the CTC coordinating with FBI authorities to formally issue a bounty on his head. The US government officially pronounced a reward in early December 1997 of $5 million for any information that would lead to the capture and/or arrest of Hafez Al-Zedicki.

All this was good news to Betts. He couldn't care less about all the accolades attributed to him and his faith in Munir. When COS Ljubjana took credit for the idea of backpacking Munir and Hamid into Armenia for sneaking into Georgia, Betts didn't try to refute it. When his intelligence reports were changed so that the credit for his reporting went to others, he didn't mind. His sole defender was his former Marine Corps Captain, Darryl Beeker, now the chief of the FBI's Joint Terrorism Task Force in New York City (NY/FBI/JTTF). Supervisory Special Agent Beeker uploaded a brief message to Betts on his communications system and had it securely transferred to the CIA's Direct Message system for employees working at remote sites. Betts got a call one afternoon from the communications section at the Addis Ababa station advising him that he had a special message. When he got in, the bemused communications officer handed him the note:

TOP SECRET – ADDIS ABABA ONLY
FROM SECRET – NY/FBI/JTTF

To: Randall Betts, Ethiopia:
"Congratulations and Good Luck Fighting With Those Army

Bayonets. If You Came Through This Ordeal, You Would Age With Dignity. Semper Fi."

The commo officer looked for the knowing smile on Betts's face. When it came, he had to ask, "So what's all that about? Some code?"

"Yeah," said Betts happily, "But not a secret code. Army bayonets are considered paper weights when compared to USMC ka-bar knives. He's telling me to watch out for the lightweights who try to push us around."

"Roger that," said the commo officer, a former technical specialist from the US Navy. "What's the other sentence about? I know, it's none of my business, but it's a pretty unusual remark."

Betts regarded the note for a moment and dropped his voice a bit.

"It is a quote by William Manchester, an author who served in the Pacific. He was my inspiration to join the Corps in the first place."

"Cool, so the semper fi thing is the marine corps motto, right?" said the younger tech expert.

"My former commanding officer trying to cheer me up," Betts said as he handed the paper back to the commo officer. This message could not leave the commo room. It would be ground into tiny shards and placed in a special bag for burning in the embassy's basement furnace.

Betts walked out of the commo room, through the heavy doors of the CIA station spaces, and passed the marine security guards in the embassy's front lobby before stepping outside and feeling the sun on his face.

***

Betts was reborn. He was jubilant that somebody had taken the time to reach out and offer some support. Those few words meant the world to him. Now he was going to find Munir and punish the fuckers who killed Hamid. But first, he was going to call Denise. His courage and faith renewed, he wanted to hear her voice just one more time.

Two days after the shooting in the Pankisi Gorge, the Georgian Security Service swept through the camp identified by Bondo Georgadze and found empty shacks and tents and a lone body later identified as Hamid Afridi. His torn body had been covered with leaves and branches, but the colorful canteen around his neck had alerted the Georgians to his final resting place.

After some brief discussions with the US Embassy, the Georgian Security Service released Hamid's body—along with his canteen and the Polaroid of him and his family—to the state department for shipping to Islamabad and then by an independent shipping company to his family in Chitral. No note or recognition or condolence letter was attached to the remains. COS Tbilisi asked COS Islamabad to pass along some statement of regret over the loss of Hamid to the family, but no such statement could be made. Any sign of attributing Hamid to the US Embassy would damage Munir's cover, so it was agreed that the body would simply appear at the Afridi doorstep, courtesy of the Pakistani ISID.

On the same day that the independent shipper left Islamabad with the sealed remains of Hamid Afridi for shipment to his family in Chitral, an employee of the US Embassy took a two-week leave of absence. It was spring of 1996, and the employee, a low-level mail clerk named James A. Brewer, had petitioned for leave to allow him to visit various parts of Pakistan and study its culture. Brewer's travel plans, which had to be submitted for approval by the ambassador, included some of the more beautiful parts of the country such as Swat Valley, Mohmand Province (where some of the finest marble in the world was mined), and Chitral. Brewer noted on his request for travel that he was looking forward to seeing the Kalash Spring Festival in Chitral.

Chapter Twelve

The Kalash Festival is a vibrant display of arts and crafts in a remote area of the Federally Administered Tribal Area (FATA). The residents of the various villages gather to set up tables and tents and dance areas to exhibit the great artistic skills handed down for generations. The prices are not cheap for the bowls and vases, and the numerous beverages for consumption may not be the best one can find in the modern world, but nothing matches the experience of seeing the marvelous colors and textures and folk art available. All through the open field used for the festival, local musicians and dancers give the festival a pleasing and active environment. The engineering and architecture involved in building the residences vertically against the steep hillsides of this part of the country was a stunning tribute to man adapting to his environment.

In this swirl of ancient culture and modern world marketing stood Jim Brewer at the far end of the festival field, keeping an eye on one of the residences arrayed at the bottom of a steep bluff.

Brewer had traveled here by bus and hired car, an altogether uncomfortable ride in very unhospitable areas that took a week to accomplish. He found the hospitality to be genuine at the road houses where he stopped to rest, but the neighborhoods did not always have a good vibe. COS Islamabad had allowed Brewer to check out a Glock Model 19 handgun, and he kept it close and ready at all times.

But he made it. The final leg was a small plane that landed him in Chitral at the craziest landing strip he had ever seen. The pilot literally landed on a runway on a downhill slant of over fifteen degrees, and it was a nerve-racking bang and brake-lock that got them stopped. When they did stop, Brewer could see that the plane was fifty feet from the end of the runway, and the drop-off into the valley beyond that was too steep to look over. The pilot assured him the takeoff would be much smoother.

Now he was walking among the festival merchants, watching the Afridi house. Brewer had checked the address and confirmed with a merchant that the Afridi family lived there. He had intentionally arrived on the day that the sealed container was due to arrive here, and he wanted to pass along the condolences of Betts and the US government for the loss of their boy. And he had money for the family. They might throw it in his face, they might chase him off with a gun, but he was going to make the effort.

As a state trooper back in Virginia, one of the most difficult tasks assigned to them would be a death notice. A traffic fatality or an accident that resulted in someone's death would initiate orders for a state trooper, hopefully accompanied by a family friend or clergy member, to report the death to the immediate family. Brewer knew all too well that a parent's reaction to the drunk-driving death of their cherished child could be erratic and world-ending. He hated that duty, and his status as a master trooper meant that the task fell to him way too often. Today, this duty fell to him as well, and he drew a sharp breath as a large cargo truck pulled into the village.

Brewer eased a bit as he assessed the truck. These three-ton lorries that carried everything from lumber to caged chickens were gaudily dressed in colors and fringes and decals that made them highly visible. Called *jinga trucks*, they were a source of both trust and jokes for their reliability and their outlandish patterns. Brewer relaxed himself by guessing that this truck was part of the festival. Indeed, it blended in with all the garish artwork. But then the truck pulled up just beyond the front door of the Afridi residence, and the passenger climbed out and walked to the front door.

Brewer wanted to go over right away and help pass the word

to the family, but he knew he had to hold off until the truck left. No way could he expose the US Embassy condolences in front of the delivery crew. That news would be spread all over the FATA by the next morning.

Once the front door was answered, two people stepped from the residence at the beckoning of the truck's passenger. A typically dressed Kalasha woman and a stooped but chiseled man stepped to the back of the truck while the driver climbed out to release the tailgate and slide the container out of the truck bed. The passenger was mildly gesturing to the sealed box sitting at the edge of the tailgate, and with a quick gesture, the box was unceremoniously dropped from the truck onto the ground.

The scream of anguish and panic was immediate and frightening. Brewer thought he had heard all the female cries of grief, but this was different. This was a cascade of anger and remorse and agony that resembled a battle cry more than a show of sorrow. When that cry was heard, the music and the dancers in the festival stopped, and Brewer found himself surrounded by dozens of residents looking at the same scene: Ashta Afridi wailing in grief.

Instantly the stooped man, presumably the father of Hamid Afridi, jumped toward the man who had motioned for the casket to be dropped from the truck. For the weathered old body that he appeared to have, he suddenly lurched onto the other man with a rapid fury that Brewer would not have anticipated. The man who ordered the casket dropped, a well-dressed but somewhat obese Pakistani in pristine clothes, did not appear to be a traditional workman. He stepped back from the sudden attack of the Afridi man but quickly produced a small knife and slashed across the older man's face. This caused the Afridi man to fall back while clutching his face, as the well-dressed man then produced a small pistol and began to point it at the Afridi woman.

Jim Brewer was there in an instant. Running as he drew his Glock pistol from a concealment pocket in his backpack, Brewer shouted at the man holding a pistol ten feet from the wailing face of a grieving mother. The man turned and pointed his pistol at Brewer with full confidence that he was controlling the situation. Brewer stopped short to hold his pistol at full extension, ready to fire. But when he noticed that the truck driver had grabbed an AK-47 rifle from the truck's bed and was pointing it in his direction, Brewer had to reassess his situation.

As the Afridi man was lying on the ground reeling from the open cut to his face, he stayed down in an attempt to stanch the flow of blood. As the Afridi woman stared at the sight of her husband on the ground and the armed threat that had just pointed away from her, she stood paralyzed. Then the truck driver reaffirmed his grip on his rifle and clicked off the safety. He now stood a bit taller, a bit more ready to fire on Brewer. The well-dressed Pakistani man with the pistol pointed at Brewer's stomach spoke.

"You have made an unwise choice, my friend. You are interfering with government business. This family has been formally notified of the death of their relative, and under Sharia law they have less than twenty-four hours to bury the body. And I am the enforcement of law in this area, so their grief is of little importance to me. As are you."

As Brewer stood still with his Glock raised, he noticed a small flourish of movement just to the armed man's right. It wasn't enough to take Brewer's eyes off his soon-to-be assailant, but it was a flourish, nonetheless.

Ashta Afridi drew a ceremonial dagger from under her sweater and moved to the obese body of the armed man with a quickness that was difficult to observe. She held the knife high at her shoulder, ran it straight and quick into the right side of her target's head. The tip of the knife came in just below the man's ear and behind the jawline, and the rest of the knife was plunged in with an exaggerated straight line shove from Ashta's hand. With the two-inch wide body of the blade going into his brainstem, Senior ISID Agent Hamza Khattack died before he dropped his pistol and fell to the ground.

Brewer was now in panic mode as he swung his Glock to attain the second target, the driver standing confidently pointing an AK-47 rifle at him from the back of the truck. The driver had turned his head quickly to witness the killing of the ISID agent that had paid him, but he turned his attention back to the stranger holding a gun on him. Brewer was struggling to hold the pistol still when the driver's chest suddenly exploded, and he fell back into the bed of truck.

Just then Brewer heard a rifle shot behind him as the AK-47 clattered back onto the bed. Brewer spun around quickly but drew his pistol back to a protracted position against his chest. The Glock 9-mm was ready to be used but not pointed at anyone or anything. Brewer searched the crowd that had gathered at the sight of the confrontation. They all stared with a knowing look of recognition and resignation. They had seen such violence all too often, and this was just another demonstration of frontier justice.

Brewer kept looking for someone to lower a rifle, someone to step up to help, someone to acknowledge what had just happened. But they all turned away and returned to the festival. Nothing to see here; nobody saw anything. A shot had come from the crowd, a powerful but accurate shot, and nobody claimed responsibility. The music and dancing resumed.

It took Brewer a few moments to comprehend what just happened, but the soft cries of Ashta Afridi brought him back. He turned back toward the residence to see Ashta stooped in front of her home tending to her husband's cut as he laid on the ground. She was speaking in a soothing, Urdu tone, telling him that he was fine, that the cut was bleeding but not deep, and that she would go inside and retrieve gauze for his wound, all while she had tears and a runny nose. She stood and went inside as Badshaw Afridi sat upright and held a small piece of cloth against his face.

Brewer put his pistol away and stepped up slowly to within a few feet of the chiseled, slight frame of the fierce-looking Pashtun. He knelt to be face-to-face with Badshaw and motioned with his hand in a sympathetic gesture so as to communicate with him.

Badshaw glanced at the foreigner who had come to his aid and calmly said, "My wife has gone for a bandage. I'll be fine."

The English statement shocked Brewer a bit, but he leaned in to do his duty.

"Mr. Afridi, sir, I have come to offer my condolences on the death of your boy Hamid. Please know that we are very sorry for your tragic loss, and I have come to pass along some things that might be of interest."

"What can you bring that would be of interest to us?"

A sharp, low reply came from behind him. Ashta Afridi had come from the house with a small towel and was pressing it against her husband's wrinkled face before Brewer could answer. Her face was clear but her look of loathing for Brewer was the same as she had shown for the man she stabbed. Her eyes held the passion and fire of the warrior caste in this part of the world, but her colorful clothing and soothing attention to Badshaw told a different story.

"Mrs. Afridi," Brewer suddenly remembered that he was still wearing his Washington Nationals ball cap and snatched it from his head. "My name is Brewer, I work for the US government, and I came here from the embassy to pass along our condolences and update you on Munir."

At this, the look of despising and grief and disinterest dropped from both of their faces, and they turned expectantly at Brewer. The uncertainty was there, as though Jim Brewer had come to deliver two death notices, but they peered straight into his eyes now.

"Munir is safe and alive. Hamid died at the hands of an evil group that is plotting death and destruction against my people, and Munir has helped us stop them."

The forced breaths and closed eyes of both the Afridis convinced Brewer that he didn't have to say any more about Munir's help to the US' they just wanted to hear about Munir's safety. After being welcomed into their small, tidy home, Brewer tried to calm their anxious questions about where their youngest son was and where he had been. He had to keep Munir safe and excluding as much information as he could, even from his parents, was critical to that mission.

"What may we offer you? Dates, fruit, bread? I make the bread myself," gushed Ashta as she sat Brewer at the kitchen table.

"I am fine, Mrs. Afridi. I had a large breakfast in Derai next to the Swat River before my journey here." Brewer said. He had almost lost that breakfast upon landing in Chitral.

"You come here from Islamabad?" asked Badshaw, his eyes laser focused on Brewer. The elder Pashtun was apprising the young man who had come to his aid. His bandaged nose and cheek could not hide the sharp eyes and furrowed brow of a worried father.

"Yes sir, Randy Betts wrote to me and begged me to come out here to tell you that Munir is alive, and we are doing all we can to keep him safe."

"Who?" asked Ashta Afridi. Her question had both curiosity and concern. She was caught by the phrase "doing all we can."

"Folks, Munir met up with one of the finest officers I know. Randall Betts is honest, forthright, and dedicated to stopping these Islamic radicals everywhere. He learned a lot from Munir about how they are funneling young men throughout Europe to fight crazy wars against the West and getting them killed for almost no reason!"

Brewer stopped abruptly. He had forgotten that he was not in a ranch-style home in Culpeper Virginia and that these folks might not take kindly to his American opinion about Islamic terrorists.

Badshaw then leaned in.

"That's how they killed our firstborn, Munir's brother, Azzam. Leading him down to Peshawar with promises of great fights and glorious victory. All for nothing, He is dead."

Badshaw sat back straight and lightly touched the bandages on his face. Even though Ashta told him to leave the bandages alone, Badshaw was starting to feel the throb of the cut.

Brewer took a moment to soak that in. He thought back to the extensive records he looked up in response to Betts's trace request on Munir Afridi. Brewer had learned a lot about the family, and this last phrase caught him.

"Azzam?" said Brewer looking to Badshaw and back to Ashta. "But he's alive!"

Ashta rose to her feet quickly and spoke with a voice filled with sadness and anger. Badshaw just held his stare on this American.

"ISID told us. That pig Khattack told us he was dead! The one I stabbed just now. He told us two years ago that Azzam had been killed fighting the Russians in Afghanistan."

Her open stare and strained voice required a light touch from Brewer.

"Well," said Brewer as he folded his fingers together on the table, "our guys in Peshawar report that he has been working in Mohmand Province, just North of the Khyber Pass, mining marble for the Taliban."

The Afridis looked to one another and then back to Brewer. Their shock and surprise and look of hopeful joy had made this whole miserable trip worthwhile.

"You have brought us our sons," said Badshaw Afridi. Nothing else came out of the older man's mouth. He simply sat back in his chair, closed his eyes and folded his sturdy, wrinkled hands across his chest. His wife went to the door and started shouting orders to other residents about hiding the truck and disposing of the two open bodies, and then she went about assembling some neighbors to help her prepare a gravesite for Hamid. She was happy that this American had come to report these things, but he had to leave right away so that she could cry again.

Part Three

Chapter Thirteen

17 December 1997
Adis Ketema neighborhood, Addis Ababa, Ethiopia

"You don't have anything there. Just forget it, and get back here. We have more important things for you to do," the CTC department head at CIA headquarters had said into the secure phone.

It had been over a year, and nothing had materialized of Munir's threat information. They had been unable to locate Munir through the cheap phone he had been provided in Bosnia, and the local service had turned up nothing in months of surveillance over the little café. The repair shop was a dry hole, and none of the routes that Munir spoke about had turned up any sign of Hafez Al-Zedicki. It was as if the master terrorist and Munir the asset had fallen off the face of the earth.

The embassies in Ethiopia, Kenya, and Tanzania had been alerted, and the rise in the threat status had allowed the State Department to increase the size of the Marine Security Guard contingent at each site. More strenuous attention was given to visitors and packages coming to the embassy, and employees were cautioned to be vigilant as they kept their busy schedules. In all, hundreds of thousands of dollars were spent to raise the security level. None of it resulted in any evidence of a terrorist threat.

And now the second-guessing came: one after another, experts in the intelligence community began to forget about Munir or doubt the veracity of his information. Senior officials and congressional oversight committees that were begging for scraps of information a year ago were now telling the director of central intelligence that CIA's golden boy was a fluke, that he had struck out. The "incredible source" was probably dead somewhere. A waste of time and money, they had said. Maybe, some had opined, Betts was making all this up.

That hit Betts hard as he drove around the dark, wet streets of Addis Ababa. The rainy season had been right on schedule, and the urgently needed rainfall turned the dusty, dry streets into muddy paths. But it matched Betts's mood perfectly. He had been searching eagerly for Munir for months, and now his management was turning against him just as the streets became slick and dangerous. As he passed a bank of pay phones, he saw that many of them were available. Normally these public phones would be swamped with eager callers, but the rainy weather and the advent of cheaper, more reliable cell phones made public phones a thing of the past. Betts wanted to call Denise, but convinced himself that listening to another unanswered call would depress him even further.

He was being recalled to Washington. His department chief had been careful to remain passive in his message, but the intent was clear: we can't trust you anymore, and you must return to face the music. A small, clustered office of workstations and sparse furniture in the CIA's basement awaited him, maybe an office next to that prick who sent him out to Jordan years earlier. Betts didn't care about all that; he just wanted to know where Munir was, that he was at least alive.

Betts had received word from Jim Brewer about the delivery

of Hamid's body to Munir's family last year, but nothing about the *incident* with the ISID agent. Brewer had crafted a very detailed report about his travels, ending with a portion dedicated to his visit with the Afridis. Brewer advised that they had been both saddened about Hamid's loss and delighted to know that Munir had not been harmed and asked nothing about his connection to the US Embassy (which was true).

Brewer reported that he had made contact with the Afridis after Hamid's body had been delivered (which was true), and his initial report ended with two paragraphs: one advising the CIA that he had not divulged any operational information pertaining to Munir's work with Betts, and the other documenting that he had received a signed receipt for the operational payout made to the Afridis. Unbeknownst to the intelligence community, this was the final portion of the report. COS Islamabad made Jim Brewer remove that paragraph about the $10,000 payout before he released the cable, as it would cause more attention than needed.

As Betts thought about Brewer's report and smiled again as he recalled that Brewer had confided the other parts of the story to a field engineer so that he could pass it to Betts without any written exposure, something caught his eye.

Half of a block up from where Betts was negotiating the mud and the throngs of people in the street moving from the bus station, something was hanging from a traffic sign. Betts turned the windshield wiper motor a click higher so he could get a better look and was rewarded with confirmation; something had been hung high on a sign that was facing the street he was driving on. He drew up to the sign post to get a better look and swallowed hard as he craned his neck to see.

Attached to a metal post in the sidewalk was a sign about seven feet off the ground, advising pedestrians that it was unsafe to cross here and encouraged them to cross at the intersection. Laying across the sign high up and telling people something they ignored was a faded canteen that had once been colorful. Even in the rain and dark Betts could see that it had been weathered from weeks of open sunlight, and the sight of it thrilled him to no end. It was Munir's signal; he had been here for some time and had not left yet.

***

Forty hours later the surveillance operation had been moved six blocks from the TV repair shop to a third-floor office overlooking the street where the canteen hung. Betts could not get anything closer, as the street-level shop belonged to a barber, and the second floor was the office of a prominent attorney. The third floor was the best he and the security service could do, but it was the top floor, and some coverage from the rooftop was available. Betts stood in the small office overlooking the street. He wouldn't take a chance of being seen on the roof.

"My men are in position and ready to move in," the federal police captain said to Betts.

"In position? We don't know anything about the place—where they're staying, how many are in there—we need to gather some information first!"

Betts was in the middle of a sweet cake he had snagged from the restaurant on the first floor where the previous surveillance had been set up. The owner was sorry to see all the people leave, as he was counting on the extra money from the rent of his upstairs apartment.

"Does not matter. We have the men, and we have surprise. Wherever they are in that apartment building, and however many of them are in there, we can handle it!" The captain was eager to get this operation over with.

Just then one of the NISS agents who had been watching the front of the building through binoculars called out, "Somebody's coming out!"

The three men craned against the window to see a single male walk out of the apartment building and turn to his right, moving along the sidewalk in a natural, unrushed manner. Betts dropped his cake and swallowed hard. No mistaking, even with the longer hair. It was Munir.

"That's my man! That's Soloman!" said Betts quickly. Munir's picture had been shared with the NISS and the Federal Police, but the name given was Soloman Deressa. This was to protect Munir's true identity, and using the name of a famous Ethiopian poet might help soothe any impulse to harm him during an arrest.

"What's he doing?" asked the young agent behind the binoculars.

Munir had stopped to peer into a store front window, and as he looked into the glass, he used his left hand to shield the glare from his eyes while he placed his right hand flat on the window, straight out from his body with his fingers splayed out: he was signifying FIVE.

"That's the apartment number! Number five is on the second floor!" said the captain suddenly.

"Maybe he's telling us that there are five guys in the apartment!" was Betts's response.

"How do we know he's saying anything at all?" said the young security service agent. He was the bright one in the room, untouched with a connection to Munir, and not in a hurry to conduct a raid that could prove disastrous.

Before Betts could begin to answer, the police captain turned to two of his men who had been standing in the office doorway and issued curt, hurried orders. The two men scurried down the steps while broadcasting into their radios.

"What are you doing?" pleaded Betts. "We don't know anything yet. Give me a chance to talk with—"

"No," said the captain firmly. "This is my country and my city. You give no orders here!"

Betts was in the middle of responding to this dangerous sentiment when he heard screams and shouts and saw six uniformed men with rifles rush the front door while a second unit of six uniformed men pushed people on the sidewalk aside as they rushed down to alley to the back of the building.

The shouts, shots, and radio broadcasts that followed would haunt Betts for the rest of his life. The captain had walked slowly down the stairs, coolly answering radio calls and issuing orders. The raid was over in five minutes, and a police wagon pulled up in front of the apartment building as marked cars closed off both ends of the street. The only vehicles allowed onto that block were ambulances. Betts counted three when he looked down the right side of the street. Out from the front of the building, five men in various stages of dress were led out onto the sidewalk. They wore hoods over their heads, and the blood on the hoods was obvious. Each man had his hands tied behind his back, and they were lashed together with a firm rope. They carried several open wounds and walked unsteadily to the back of the police wagon and were loaded into the back by a dozen policemen.

As horrible was this scene was, Betts could not look away. The information that could have been available from these men was now worthless due to the treatment they had faced from the police. That made Betts look up to the left direction of the street where Munir had been standing, but he was unable to see him. Where Munir had been looking through the glass window was a group of police officers holding someone on the sidewalk. The person being held down by the men was not clear, but the shattered window where Munir had been standing told Betts who it was.

Betts and the young NISS agent bolted from the office and cleared the stairs into the street. They ran up to the scene just as Munir was being stood up by at least five federal policemen dressed all in black. Munir's face was bloody, and his shirt was torn.

Betts waded into the small crowd of policemen as the young security service agent behind him announced in Ethiopian his affiliation and that this man would be taken separately. It was then that Betts felt a jolt he had not felt since his training at Parris Island; a policeman slightly taller than Betts shoved him and the young agent onto their backs on the sidewalk. It was an incredibly fast, effective blow from the policeman's right elbow that instantly pushed Betts back, and the force of the hit transferred into the young man behind him. They were left stunned, sitting up on the sidewalk.

With enough space being created by this action, the policeman then whipped his FN FNC rifle off his shoulder and leveled it at Betts. The policeman said two distinct sentences and joined with his colleagues as they handcuffed Munir and led him roughly to the police wagon.

"What did he say?" Betts said as he caught his breath and turned to stand up.

"He said that if you get up off the sidewalk before they leave, he will shoot you and drag your body into the street to be run over by the police wagon," came the reply from the young agent as he held Betts down by his shoulder.

***

When Betts did get up from the sidewalk, he made three phone calls as he and the young security agent headed back to his car. The first call was to the chief of the National Security Service, telling him what happened and complimenting the work of his NISS staff. The chief promised that he would call police headquarters and chew somebody out for the hasty action. The second call was to the Office of Presidential Security. During the last few months, Betts had worked with the protection service for the president (mostly about physical security measures), and they had always reminded him that any help he needed would be quickly handled. Betts explained to the protection detail leader (PDL) what had happened to him and his *good friend*, and the PDL promised that he would have the man released within the hour. These were not *whining* in Betts eyes, as much work had been done with the various national security organs in this country to improve their ability to preserve stability and a positive image to the world. This hastily arranged raid and the mistreatment of Munir had to be addressed quietly, and getting the top officials to respond was the best way to rectify the issue.

The third call he made was to his CIA station management. As Betts maneuvered through the busy streets of the capitol, he spoke with his operations chief and then to the station chief himself. As the young NISS agent was being dropped off at his headquarters, Betts was receiving one of the most mixed-message ass chewings ever.

"Are you injured? Are you safe now?" asked the ops chief.

"I'm fine, I'm driving over to the jail to pick up my guy now." Betts avoided giving any names, especially now.

"Negative, negative, negative," came the reply. "You have to stay out of this mess altogether. The second that the police took over the situation, you should have backed out and called the office. You have breached so many layers of protocol here that it will be difficult to keep you in country."

"Look, this guy needs our help! Without some intervention, who knows what will happen to him!" Betts was getting fed up with this conversation. His chief of ops was running hot and cold on him, and the lack of support for Munir and what he had done was frustrating.

"What happens to him is what happens to him. We can't be showing our hand on this, and your allegiance is supposed to be to this office, not some terrorist caught up in a police raid!" said the ops chief with an increasingly indifferent tone. "We spend a lot of time nurturing our liaison relationships here, and you're ruining that for the sake of some street kid."

"Fuck you," said Betts. He'd had all he could have of this. "Do you have any idea how much we've collected from this *street kid*?"

"You can't talk to me like that mister. Now you will—"

Betts hung up the phone. He was pulling into the rear entrance of the justice center, the holding and booking facility for most police actions in the capitol. Nothing else would be accomplished with this conversation, and Betts had to hurry. He jumped out of his car and approached the main doors to the booking area. He waited for someone to walk out before he could grasp the heavy door and get himself inside.

What he saw inside was a sordid madhouse. In every square foot of the large lobby area, people scuffled with police officers or slept on the wooden benches along the old, grimy walls. Betts tried to make his way through the mass of chaos and shouts as suspects were hauled in front of a desk for processing by jail staff who looked meaner than the criminals in front of them. The floors were slick with various liquids, some of them body fluids, some of them from tear gas that preserved a stinging stench in the air. This was no place to be for more than a minute.

"Mr. Betts!" came a call from the far end of the lobby. Betts looked through the crowd to see a small, thin man in a black suit and tie standing in front of two heavy doors and waving him over. When he finally got to where the man was standing, the man had pulled a black leather wallet from his suit coat and showed Betts his badge.

"Chief Inspector Ngebe with the National Security Service," he said over the din in the lobby. "My boss said you'd need some help getting a suspect released."

"Glad you're here," said Betts as he shook the man's hand. "I don't know where he is, but he came in less than an hour ago."

"The raid in Ketema? Those guys are still being questioned," said Ngebe.

"Well, I need to get him out of there. He wouldn't have anything valuable to the police," lied Betts. He would have plenty of information, but it needed to go to CIA, not a bunch of thugs in the back room of a police station.

As Ngebe was processing this, the heavy doors behind him swung open, and the police chief who had initiated the raid walked through. He said a few curt lines to Inspector Ngebe then continued on with a cutting look at Betts. Behind him, the large policeman in the black outfit who had elbowed Betts to the sidewalk walked with a defiant stare at the two men. It was clear to Betts that they had been briefed on Munir's importance.

"So, we can pick him up now?" Betts said expectantly.

"The decision has been made to allow you to brief this man, but he will not be released until the others that were collected in the raid are," said Ngebe carefully.

Betts tried not to show his frustration with this decision.

"I thought you would be coming down here to get him released!"

Ngebe looked at Betts with a slight smirk on his face.

"I was sent here to keep you from being thrown into the cell with him! That raid caused a lot of trouble for the police chief, and he is being lowered in rank because he rushed in, causing a lot of broken doors and shot-up residents. They went to two other apartments with families before they found the right apartment, and by the time they got there, the terrorists were ready. Two policemen and an innocent resident were shot. So they're not turning this man loose anytime today."

"I begged him not to go in that soon," Betts said.

"We know, but the magistrate has been briefed by our office, and he says that a full investigation is warranted and releasing your man, whose name is NOT what you told us, would be harmful to that investigation."

Betts had nowhere to go on that one. He had no options here; his only access to Munir would be in a police interrogation room.

"May I at least talk with him alone?" Betts asked. "Of course," Ngebe said, demonstrating as much deference as he could. "I shall get a room cleared for you."

Chapter Fourteen

Later the same day.
Addis Ababa City Administration Police Commission, Lideta,
Ethiopia.

Munir had been handled roughly before, but never with this ferocity. The cut in his forehead from being pushed into the glass store front window had stopped bleeding, but it was throbbing now. And the welt on his right cheek from the butt of the policeman's rifle was swelling to a point that it started inhibiting his sight in that eye. But these were trivial to the bruises he incurred once he had been arrested. It seemed that the police were intent on breaking something as they *processed* him at the police station. In between interviews with the police, Munir was placed in a community cell with brightly painted green walls and overlapping smells of urine and body odor. The two dozen or so men in the cell mostly sat on the wooden benches along the walls or on the floor. Very few of them paced the floor, and the conversations were quiet. He was almost glad that his swollen nose required him to breathe through his mouth, as the competing stench was stiff in the air. As Munir leaned against the back wall of the cell on a wooden bench, he became aware of a person sitting down on his left. Fearing that this was another attempt to push him around or force him from his seat, Munir looked over with his one good eye to see an older man in a faded robe sitting close to him.

"I see that you have become acquainted with the police," said the old man in a soft, almost soothing tone. His language was Arabic, and he spoke slowly and clearly. Munir was grateful for the nonalerting approach, but still mindful of the possible threat by the myriad of criminals herded into this cell. He simply turned away from looking at this kindly old man.

"Tell me, why are they singling you out for punishment? What terrible crime did you commit?" asked the old man.

Munir finally found an answer, "They believe that me not being a Muslim is a worse crime than consorting with criminals."

Munir heard the older man chuckle, and then he felt the faint touch of a warm, smooth hand on his arm. "Those who suffer for their faith are blessed above all," said the man in a voice somewhat stronger than before. He was clearly a cleric or priest.

"I have been raised in a house that studies all religions, and I respect Islam, but I have not dedicated my life to a faith that teaches hate and rejection of other religions," answered Munir. He didn't know why he entrusted this stranger with his inner feelings about religion, but he felt that he could relax with this man.

The old man looked earnestly at Munir and began, "Young man, you have been ill-informed. Islam emphasizes self-awareness, self-discipline, and the struggle against negative tendencies. Inner peace is achieved by purifying the heart from hatred, jealousy, and other harmful emotions and by seeking contentment and gratitude. Islamic teachings encourage mindfulness and meditation on the remembrance of Allah, which brings serenity and tranquility to the soul." As Munir looked to the man while he spoke, he saw a grace and genuine honesty that he had rarely seen before. This man was speaking directly into Munir's heart, and it made Munir turn in his seat to face him.

"You are a man of faith?" Asked Munir sheepishly.

The old man grinned and looked down, "I am but a simple servant of the *ummah*.

Munir looked quizzically at him; he had never heard this term before. The older man continued, "It is the global community of believers that encourages cooperation, mutual support, and peace among diverse peoples and cultures."

"Why have I never heard these things before?" Munir was starting to see that his education about various religions may not have been very extensive.

"Because we hear so many things these days which are misguided and confused. The Prophet teaches that *dhimma*, the Islamic law that protects the rights of nonMuslim minorities, grants them religious freedom and autonomy. This spirit of tolerance contributed to the coexistence of diverse communities in many Islamic societies."

"They don't seem to believe that here," said Munir flatly.

"Governments concern themselves with preserving their power. Those who seek peace and faith are a force that no government can conquer. Always remember that you are braver than you believe, and stronger than you seem." said the man in a stern and clean tone that surprised Munir.

This was a source of information that encouraged Munir to share more about himself and his background. This plain-looking man with a gentle accent and a solid speaking voice was a representative of a monotheistic culture that showed a patience and righteousness that worked to restore Munir's inner strength. Suddenly, he didn't feel the oppressive weight of his injuries upon him.

As Munir leaned closer to the old man to speak further, the cell door opened with a creak, and two jailers came in. They lifted Munir by his underarms and carried him roughly out of the cell. As they locked the cell door back and hussled Munir down the hall, he could hear the old man reciting an Islamic prayer.

Once Munir was dragged from the community cell he was taken to a room in another part of the building.

Once the room door was opened, Munir was pushed in and the door was slammed shut behind him. The room was small and poorly lit; it had no windows and no mirror, just a video camera placed high in the far corner and a table and two chairs. In one of the chairs was Betts. Munir breathed a bit of relief; he did not expect the American to beat him.

"Long way from Pankisi Gorge," said Betts quietly as he helped Munir to the other chair. A bottle of water was on the table, and Betts slid it across the table as he sat across from his battered asset.

"I was hoping that Sergeant Krucic would come and save me," was all that Munir could say. He tried a bit of a smile, but his cheek hurt too much.

"Did you know we were watching you?" asked Betts.

"Our window overlooked the street," Munir said with a dismissive look. "You see three cops on the rooftop staring at you through binoculars, you kind of figure it out!"

"Can't tell you how sorry I am about this," started Betts. He had a speech prepared about how long he had been searching and how much he had tried to get Munir released.

Munir cut him off.

"They killed Hamid. The bastards shot him because they thought he was the one who tipped you off."

"Partner, we found Hamid, and he was transported back to your folks for proper burial, along with his canteen and the Polaroid of the family. My buddy was there when the casket arrived, the local security guy tried to get mean with your parents so he's dead. We did what we could, but your folks are overjoyed to know that you are safe and alive."

Betts tried to make his commentary to Munir as vanilla as he could, so that specific information was not overheard by the policemen observing the debrief.

As this news was relayed to Munir, the emotions welled up in him, and he lowered his head to shed stinging tears that he hoped nobody would see.

"As well as Azzam," said Betts quietly. He wanted that name to be left out of the investigation, but he needed to tell Munir that his older brother was still alive.

Munir looked up quickly from his tears at this. "Are you certain of this?"

"I am, my buddy found him. We got him some cash to travel home. Now, I need to know what you know. Can you tell me anything about the plans? About Al-Zedicki? Why hasn't he shown up here? What is the status of this bombing plot?" rattled off Betts, trying to get as much information in as short a time as possible.

"Al-Zedicki has been here and gone," Munir said flatly. "He came in through the Somaliland's Port of Bosaso. He passed out the cash to purchase the trucks, fertilizer, chemicals, and electrical switches. Everything but the explosives are stored and waiting in a garage east of the city."

Betts was dumbfounded. They had watched all the air routes and overland routes from Eritrea and Uganda, but never thought about the rarely used commercial port on the northern coast of the Horn of Africa. This would be another good lead for CTC analysts.

Munir continued as he leaned forward, trying to keep his voice low.

"The US Embassy here is on an open plain, so we have been fixing a special van with a hard shell on one side to help deflect the blast into the compound. The others in Kenya and Tanzania have enough buildings around them to make better compression. The attack is planned for March; we have been storing basic goods and getting volunteers, but Al-Zedicki won't buy the explosive materials until the last minute. The final order to assemble and undertake the operation will be given by Al-Zedicki two days before the exact time and date."

Betts was writing as furiously as he could.

"Okay, so what date in March? You mean next March, 1998, right?"

As Munir nodded and started to respond to the question, the door to the room unlocked, and two jailers walked in. One went to Munir and jerked him out of his chair, and the other did the same for Betts.

Betts objected as he was stood up and hustled to the door.

"Hey! We are in the middle of a debrief! I have permission to—"

"You have no more permission, you are no longer welcome in this country. If you resist, I will throw you into the basement and tell your ambassador that I lost you on the way to the airport!"

The curt response came from the jailer who pushed him from the room and toward the building's exit. Betts saw three more jailers standing in the hallway peering into the room, ready to take Munir back to the community cell block.

The jailer holding Betts's arm walked him out of the police building and shoved him into a federal police sedan. The jailer stayed with Betts as the sedan drove out and headed toward Lideta Airport.

At the airport, Betts was shoved out of the sedan, and once he had regained his feet and was standing on the platform in front of the airport, the policemen in the sedan drove away.

***

"I have your things here," came a voice behind Betts. He turned to see the administrative assistant to the COS, a very bright woman in her fifties who was always helpful and upbeat. She was holding Betts's jacket and a nondescript polo shirt on her right arm, and in her left hand, was an envelope packed with papers.

"What's all this? Am I really leaving?" Betts said as he looked at the crowded airport terminal.

"Headquarters' orders. You are going home. I have arranged for a local service to clean out your rented house, and they will ship everything to the storage facility in Alexandria. This is a clean shirt and the jacket you had hanging in the office, and this—" she said as she handed him everything she was holding, "—is your ticketing on Lufthansa and United Airlines through London. Your flight leaves in three hours, so I put some local money in there for you to get something to eat. Keys to your car?"

She held out her hand.

Betts dug the keys out of his pocket, told her where his car was, and promised her that his office-issued cell phone had been left locked in the vehicle.

She thanked him, wished him a good flight, and walked away. No further discussion, no explanation. Betts gathered himself and walked slowly into the mass of people that never seemed to subside here.

Chapter Fifteen

0815 hours, 19 December 1997
Dulles Airport, Virginia

Once Betts had navigated the throngs of holiday travelers coming in through the foreign arrivals terminal at Dulles Airport, he then walked into the terminal exit and was met by two people. One was a young blond woman from the CIA's office of security. She approached Betts once the man with her pointed him out. She walked up with an unhurried pace and introduced herself after showing him her badge. The man with her was Jeff Bovian, who Betts had not seen since the training op in Jordan. Evidently, Bovian was there only to identify Betts.

Bovian was smiling and genuinely glad to see Betts, and the CIA/OS woman was happy to just get driving back to HQ.

"How'd your flight go, Randy?" was the first question out of Bovian.

"My layover in London was horrible. I had to spend some good bucks to get a day room at Heathrow," was Betts's response.

"Do you know why I'm being rushed back here?"

"No idea, pal," said Bovian with a dismissive wave of his hand. "Something about your management wanting a word with you."

The drive from Dulles to the rear entrance to CIA headquarters was quiet, nothing beyond small talk about the weather. As they drove through the gate at HQ, Betts found that the CIA/OS woman had called ahead so that they would not be stopped to show their badge. As Betts didn't have his, this made his entry much quicker. The security officer drove the black Ford Explorer into the garage and parked, and the three of them walked to the closest elevator. Once inside the elevator, the CIA/OS woman asked Bovian if he knew where they were going. When he answered that he did, the woman turned to Betts and wished him a nice day as the elevator door to the third floor opened. Bovian and Betts got out and they walked to the chief of the Africa department's office. Once there, Bovian shook Betts's hand and walked back to the elevator. Betts was left standing in the hallway staring at the door.

The department chief's office door was secured with an electronic lock, and when Betts pushed the doorbell, the door buzzed and unlocked. Once inside, he was met by the chief's office manager who escorted him directly into the adjacent chief's office. She announced his arrival, and he was ushered to a seat. The chief of the Africa department thanked the office manager, and she left the two men alone.

"You can't talk to your management like that," the chief said with no preamble or greeting.

"What are you talking about?" Betts asked. He was clearly confused now.

"You used a four-letter obscenity speaking with your station operations chief. He is an essential part of CIA leadership, and you talked to him like he was some sailor in a Bangkok bathroom!"

***

Betts was beginning to explain, so that he could get this meeting over with and pass the information along about his meeting with Munir. But the department chief continued.

"It is unclear to me what kind of *Motel 6* operations you're used to in CTC, but I can assure you that the Africa department does not tolerate insubordination and the insulting of its senior leadership, understand?"

Betts barely got a nod off before the senior intelligence service official continued.

"You were told to stand down on any further meetings with our asset, and you went behind your management's back to get into a debriefing room right in police headquarters! You exposed a station asset by doing this, making him worthless to us, and you exposed our station's liaison relationship with several of the security organizations! What did you think you were going to accomplish when you tried to get our asset released? And by the way you made a lot of trouble for a local partner who is critical to our operations!"

Now Betts understood. The police chief was a regular station contact. He had notified COS of the debrief at federal police HQ and probably complained about Betts calling him out.

"Sir, I needed to get Munir out of police custody because they were going to beat him to death! I got some great information about the embassy bombing plan that I'd like to share—"

"You don't know that!" the chief spat. "And you are not sharing anything. Any information you obtained is worthless thanks to your lack of discretion. A car is waiting for you at the bottom of the steps from the front lobby. You will be escorted out of this building and driven to either Dulles Airport or the closest Metro station. I don't care which, but from this moment, your status as an employee of this organization is suspended. Sign the nondisclosure form on my office manager's desk on your way out and get lost."

The chief went back to his stack of papers, indicating that this meeting was over. Betts struggled to stand but was glad to get the hell out of that office. Stepping roughly through the office door and up to the office manager's desk, Betts was still trying to grasp the weight of what he had been told. He was handed the three-page reminder about his oath to protect CIA information and initialed the line that stated that he had been properly debriefed. His hands shook slightly as he signed, knowing that this was the end of his career with the federal service. With his security clearance revoked, nobody would hire him.

He walked out of the office into the hallway, where he was met by the same CIA/OS female agent who had brought him from Dulles Airport.

"Funny seeing you here," she said in a pleasant, almost friendly tone. "I don't know if you remember, but I'm Laurie Runyon with the office of security. Where am I taking you this time?"

"Back to Dulles, I guess," was all that Betts could muster. It was clear by the presence of the CIA/OS that he would not be allowed to communicate with CTC management and would be prevented from visiting any other office other than the interior of that black Explorer at the front entrance.

For her part, Special Agent Runyon had been given the basic parameters of this matter; she was escorting a case officer who had screwed up badly overseas and was being brought in for a final debrief. Once the debrief would be completed, she was to drive him to a transportation hub and wish him a nice day. Her main objective was to be civil and accommodating but to watch him for any sign of anxiety or criminal mischief. Runyan was experienced with these situations, as she had walked out several CIA employees in the past five years. She was trained in behavior dynamics and signs of dysfunction and armed with a 9-mm sidearm if it got too hairy. She and Betts walked through the lobby, where he could take his last look at the memorial wall of stars representing the dozens of CIA officers who had died in the line of duty. As he climbed back into the black Explorer, he wished he could die right now, even though he knew they'd never give him a star.

Later, as she drove away from the United Airlines entrance at Dulles airport, Runyan looked in the rearview mirror to see Betts turn and walk slowly into the terminal building. She felt truly sorry for the guy, as he had been quiet and cooperative. He had said something about finding a flight to Tennessee, but she didn't know if he was from there or not. All that she did know was that when she wished him a good flight and expressed hope that things would go better for him, she meant it.

As Special Agent Laurie Runyon was pulling back onto the Dulles Toll Road for the short trip back to CIA HQ, her cell phone buzzed, and the number for the director's protective staff showed on the screen. This was the office that worked protection and administrative duties for the director of the CIA, and these agents were considered to be the top of the top. This was an elite office of highly trained professionals that Runyan had hoped to join one day, and hearing from this office was both promising and troubling. She answered quickly, but before she could get her name out, the voice on the other end spoke to cut her off.

"Agent Runyon, is Betts with you?" was the rushed question from the chief of the protective staff.

"I'm sorry, who?" Laurie said. She hated to be unable to provide a quick answer, but she had no idea what the chief was asking about.

"Randall Betts, the guy you were taking off campus. Is he with you?"

"No sir, I just dropped him off at Dulles."

Runyan heard a low groan from the background; evidently this phone call was on speaker. Several people were mumbling, and a quick order was given to the DPS chief.

"Agent Runyon…Laurie," said the chief, trying to assemble himself and remain calm. "I want you to get back to Dulles right now, and I mean now, and retrieve Mr. Betts and get him back here right away. Is that clear?"

The last phrase, seeking certification that she had heard her orders clearly, was not heard by Agent Runyon. She was doing almost fifty miles per hour and had slammed on the brakes to be able to catch a median crossover that was fifty feet in front of her when she was told to return to the airport. The resounding squeal of the tires, the grind of the front suspension, and the howling responses from the Explorer's engine drowned out that last bit of the chief's statement.

The cacophony of car horns in both directions of traffic on the toll road as the Explorer fishtailed from the eastbound passing lane into the westbound one didn't make hearing anything else easy either. Runyan exited the call as she turned on the hidden red and blue emergency lights on the vehicle and blasted the siren several times as she weaved through the late morning traffic heading into Dulles Airport.

Whatever Randall Betts had done, the CIA wasn't finished with him.

Chapter Sixteen

1700 hours, 19 December 1997
Keranio Adebabay Bus Terminal, Addis Ababa, Ethiopia

At approximately the same time that Special Agent Laurie Runyon was running from her vehicle and dashing through Dulles Airport, Munir Afridi and his five compatriots were being released from police custody in the Lideta neighborhood. They walked to the closest bus station and paid for a ticket heading out of the capitol. The men walked together, but their association was not a close one. Munir had very little in common with these men; they were together only because they had selective duties over the past few weeks and carried out those arrangements with an emphasis to be low-key and unobserved. The garage rental, the acquisition of the van, the location of the chemicals and electrical parts needed—these were all accomplished with very little fanfare. The purchase of the steel plating and installing it on the right-hand side of the van's cargo area—that was the sole time they had worked together. Now the preparations for the van were complete, it was just a matter of hearing from Al-Zedicki, and everything would be quickly put into place.

As the group of six arrived at the bus terminal, the team leader spoke for the first time. "Do each of you know where to go?"

When Munir and the others nodded their heads, that's when the team leader looked at Munir and pointed a finger in his chest.

"So what did you tell them?"

Munir had been separated from the others from the start, and even though they were all released at the same time, some suspicion had arisen about why he wasn't kept with them.

"I told them that between little Israeli boys and goats, you preferred to fuck goats better."

The nervous laughter didn't last long, as the team leader, a Palestinian named Mustapha Al-Araaj, didn't appreciate the humor. So Munir went for the serious answer.

"They thought I was European because of my hair color. Then when they found out I wasn't a Muslim, they wanted me for extra practice."

Munir's brown hair, different from the dark hair of everyone else, was truly an attribute that allowed him to fit in with other nationalities. The fact that he was Kalash and not a true believer kept him in some disfavor with the group, so they readily accepted the story that he would get more beatings than they would. The mark of the rifle butt on his face proved his story.

"We will split up, take a bus in different directions for just one stop, then get off and return to the garage. Once we are back together and certain we are not being followed, I'll call for a ride to get us to Bosaso," the team leader said.

Munir said nothing, but he quietly panicked: Why are they meeting at Bosaso? How can I get word to Betts about this development? What will happen now, so close to the attack?

He knew none of these answers, and based on the way Betts had been hustled out of the room before him, he was unsure what had happened to him.

Chapter Seventeen

1000 hours, 19 December 1997
Executive Suite of the Director of CIA, Langley, Virginia

She hated having to say, "yes sir," one more time, but when you're getting chewed out by the president of the United States, you have little chance (or choice) to talk back.

CIA Director Olivia Baines Johnson was a fifth-generation resident of Washington, DC, and proud of her service to the US government, as well as her family's contributions. The incoming president had nominated her quickly, and one of the few truly bipartisan votes in Congress had confirmed her position. At thirty-three, she held the distinction of being both the first African American to hold the position of chief of the CIA and the youngest. She was a bit tired of reading that her name, given to her by parents whose defense-consulting business flourished with the signing of the 1964 Civil Rights Act, was reminiscent of the LBJ name, but that's what growing up in WDC was all about.

CIA Director Johnson finally finished her *courtesy call* from the White House, hung up on an empty line, and turned to her chief of staff, who had been sitting with other senior officials nearby during the entirety of the phone call. When your boss gets a call from the Oval Office, you know to be standing by for some orders.

The director simply said, "Where is he now?"

The chief of staff turned to the chief of the protective operations group. He quickly leaned forward.

"Special Agent Runyon is bringing Betts from Dulles Airport now," he said confidently.

"She found him?" DCIA said.

"She ran full out through the airport and found him standing in line for a flight to Nashville. She is reportedly breaking all known speed records now on the toll road to return here," replied the chief of protective programs.

"Well, get her an Exceptional Performance Award (EPA), get her a promotion, something, but get her into my garage and get Betts up here, dressed and presentable, now!" Barked DCIA. "The president has made it clear to me that a major policy initiative is on hold until this young man meets with the foreign VIP who is cooling his heels in my conference room as we speak! I want Betts here right away, I do not wish to disappoint POTUS!"

"Director, chief of Africa department is here," called her executive assistant.

"Thank you, Marge. Folks, clear the room." The DCIA said this as she sat back in her office chair. The other senior officers, thrilled that they weren't going to get a list of demands from one of the sharpest minds in the intelligence community, shuffled out quickly and quietly.

The chief of the Africa department walked in, and they exchanged pleasantries for about a minute. Then the DCIA stated flatly, "I understand you lectured a young case officer about his foul language today, and then you suspended his access to CIA?"

"Yes ma'am," the chief of the Africa said, moving slightly in his chair. "And for insubordination. He was told not to pursue an asset, and yet he did."

"Well, let me fill you in on something," said DCIA leaning forward in her chair, "I have reviewed this case officer's service record and his reporting since joining this organization. That young man has served his country with honor and a risk-taking nature that I find hard to discover in CIA these days, and since POTUS just tried to strangle me over the phone for not having him available for a foreign liaison meeting today, I'm going to make this very clear to you."

She waited until she saw the blood drain from the man's face before she spoke.

"Don't you ever fucking try to fire an employee of my CIA ever a-fucking-gain."

The chief of the Africa department was still staring at her when the executive assistant stuck her head in the door. "Ma'am, he's here."

With that, DCIA stood and excused the chief of Africa department and welcomed Betts into her office. The two men stared at each other as they passed in the large doorway.

DCIA shook Betts's hand and thanked him for coming back to the place where he still had a job. Betts was flushed with confusion but allowed a quick, "Well, you should thank that special agent! She got me here in twelve minutes!"

"Walk with me," demanded DCIA as she led him back out of her office and onto her private elevator. She pressed the button for the fourth floor and faced Betts, regarding his appearance. He looked okay; evidently, he had borrowed a tie and sport coat from somebody, but he wouldn't pass for a homeless person or a tech officer.

The door opened and the two walked briskly across the hall into a conference room normally reserved for official functions. Today the long table was empty save for two seats. The two men rose reverently when Betts walked into the room. The sharp-dressed tall African American woman who controlled the entire intelligence-gathering capabilities of the US government was ignored; both men moved to Betts and hugged him with energy.

The older of the two men stared at Betts and continued to hold his hand after a hard shake. He finally said, "I've come to thank the man who saved the life of my daughter."

The younger man stepped up and eased the older man aside, and he grasped Betts's hand, saying, "I've come to see you boss, and thank you for saving my fiancé."

It took a brief moment, but Betts recognized the younger man, and the voice, and the term *boss*. It was his student from Jordan, the hidden prince who helped him take down that shooter.

The prince then said, "Randall Betts, I'd like you to meet Malik Mohammad Cherak, the new foreign minister of Algeria."

Betts admired the man as he returned his grasp to the small, older man with peaceful eyes and a furious smile. "…and my future father-in-law."

Betts's eyes widened, and he went back to shaking the prince's hand. "Congratulations! But where is your bride-to-be? Your daughter, sir?"

Betts looked a bit unsteady, unsure of who these men were talking about.

"It was my daughter visiting the royal family of Jordan the day that the prince came to your training base," explained Cherak, "She was so frightened, but so humbled by your selfless bravery in taking down the terrorist shooter!"

Betts couldn't believe this. He looked briefly at DCIA and the other senior officers who had filed into the room to witness this event. They all gave him a thumbs-up look.

Cherak continued, "And when the US president invited me to the White House to sign this agreement, in which we will soon supply 35 percent of your country's natural gas, I told him that I would happily sign for my government, just as soon as I got to meet you!"

"You are too kind foreign minister, and I hope that you will pass my well-wishes to your daughter. She was indeed the brightest part of my day."

Betts's eyes were locked onto this man; he had paid Betts a great favor, and he remembered that girl all too well.

"I will pass along those wishes. She sees very little of her father these days," the prince said, as flashes started going off from cameras brought in by the DCIA's admin staff. These would make great photos for the CIA's new marketing concept called a Web page.

Now that Betts was a bit more relaxed, he tried to figure out a puzzle and leaned a bit closer to the prince.

"I'm not sure about something. You're a Jordanian Prince, but you're marrying an Algerian?" This evoked a polite but sincere laugh from the prince.

"I took the job as chief of Algerian Mukhabarat. My family is thrilled that I have a steady job, and if I am needed at home, I can be recalled quickly. And besides, did you see that woman?"

The two men laughed heartily as the DCIA admired the scene. She stepped in at this point to introduce herself and welcome the men to CIA HQ.

Once the introductions and promises to stay in touch were exchanged throughout the room, Foreign Minister Cherak and his chief intelligence officer were rushed downstairs into a hot-running secret service motorcade that sped them to the White House, where a deal to spend $260 million each year for the next five years was waiting on the president's desk for signature.

Once everyone had left the conference room, DCIA turned to Betts and asked, "So what do you need from me?"

"Ma'am," Betts started slowly, "I need to write a cable in CTC that outlines the planned bombing attack of US Embassies on the east coast of Africa in March of next year. My asset has informed me that the mastermind, Al-Zedicki, is using the Somali Port of Bosaso for travel in and out of Addis Ababa, where the final preparations are being made right now."

By the time Betts had finished these words, the DCIA had pulled him from the conference room and pushed him down the hallway.

"Go, get to it! Write that cable! And bring me Al-Zedicki! And bring your asset back alive! And you get back here safely; we need people like you!" she hollered as employees in the hallway stopped and stared at the sight of Betts running to an elevator as the DCIA shouted behind him.

Chapter Eighteen

26 December 1997
Port of Bosaso, Autonomous Puntland Region of Somalia

The livestock port on the high end of the Horn of Africa was a busy, efficient center of commerce. Wooden dhows with full cargo holds of sheep, cattle, and emu moved in and out of the noisy shoreline, while cranes and concrete slabs were attempting to make larger container ships a staple in the trade.

Munir had never seen such organized chaos. Shouts from shore-men loading a variety of transport vessels and whines from cable winches mixed with the never-ending sound of open bartering and trading on the shoreline. Everyone had a purpose, everyone was doing a job, and everything was getting attention. This, thought Munir, is where he belonged: a clear objective; a hardy, motivated team; and an achievable goal of loading and unloading these fascinating ships.

Everybody needed money to survive, but Munir thought, for just a moment, that he would gladly do this job for free. Even with the dirt and the noise and the smoke and the barnyard smell, this place was successful. Even if it was too far from anything. The tortuous trip from Ethiopia to Somalia had been almost two days of off-road travel that was possibly worse than any smuggling route he had taken before. Even the smooth highway travel from the capitol of Puntland to the port was littered with obstacles and oppressive heat. He was glad to be done with this trip, and dreaded having to return by the same route.

And then he felt a cold slap on his shoulder and turned to face Hafez Al-Zedicki. Munir felt the shiver, facing this man, who smiled at him and said, "So you survived your time with the police! Tell me, is my plan still safe?"

The malevolence wasn't in his voice. He sounded like he was teasing a child, but Munir knew what he was up to—assessing the possible leak for nervousness.

"I told them nothing. They knew I was just the Kefir sent for coffee and dinner. All the police got from me was the sound of my injuries," admitted Munir. All this was true. He did not have the time to tell Betts anything about this part of the plan.

Al-Zedicki laughed and smacked Munir on the shoulder.

"You are a good one! We need more people like you!"

He had chosen to keep Munir alive and part of his team because of his appearance: lots of Muslims could shave their beard and color their hair to change the way they looked, but this Afridi boy had good height and posture, and his eyes and hair color were lighter than his other believers. Munir could get into places that Al-Zedicki could not. He would make good cover for the plan; he could drive 1,000 kilograms of explosives right up the crusader's ass, and they would never suspect him. When the time came, Munir would prove himself worthy.

"So, what are we doing here? Isn't everything in Addis?" asked Munir weakly.

Al-Zedicki looked off for a moment before answering.

"You and the others will be cover for me to move the final piece into Addis. I have decided that purchasing the fertilizer and ammonium nitrate chemicals in Ethiopia was too dangerous. And besides, I will not fail again like I did in New York. The bomb there was too small, so I brought one myself!"

With that statement, Al-Zedicki pointed to a small container ship jostling to get aside the port facility. The ungainly old ship looked huge next to the wooden dhows, but it was being pushed against the concrete dock a little too fast. Al-Zedicki raised his arms and shouted at the harbormaster as he ran from Munir's side and toward the ship.

"So he's not getting the materials in Addis," Munir said to Al-Araaaj as he came next to him.

"That was always the plan. He told us to scout out vendors for the materials, but that was in case he couldn't get this monster here," Al-Araaj said as he watched the master planner shout at the dock workers to be careful with the huge rusting hulk of a transport.

Munir just watched. This was very different from what he had told the American. He hoped that Betts would adjust if needed to stop this plan. And then he thought about Betts. Where was he now? Back in America, there was little Betts could do to stop this madman. The only person who could interfere with Al-Zedicki's plan now was himself. Munir tried to think of a way out of this, but without Betts's help it seemed that nobody could stop this attack.

Chapter Nineteen

One day earlier, 25 December 1997
The outer hull of an American submarine, Seawolf class, location,
name and tail number classified

The SEAL unit had squeezed into their seating locations in the delivery vehicle, checked their air supply one more time, and given a
quick audio check between them. The unit navigator, a navy commander with eight years of service in naval special warfare, pushed
the thumb button connected to the radio.

"Sunny Rock, this is Turtle. Ready to jump."

The submarine's executive officer, standing in the communication
room of one of the fastest attack submarines in the navy replied to
the man sitting in the cumbersome pod attached to the dry dock
shelter on the hull of his ship.

"Turtle, this is Sunny Rock. Good hunting,"

The unit's SEAL Delivery Vehicle (SDV) slowly lifted from the
outer hull just behind the sail and began its careful, quiet glide into
the Somali harbor of Bosaso. They had made this trip several times

in the past, normally to quietly approach pirate vessels operating off the east coast of Africa. This time, instead of planting mines onto the pirate's cargo vessels or ramming harpoons into the hulls of the dinghies to create a leak, they were instructed to come ashore quietly, observe the shipping traffic, and report back any human passengers arriving rather than livestock. Anything unusual was the secondary mission, but the sole intent was to approach, observe, and advise. No engagement was requested. Unless it was. So the SEALs were ready for anything.

Their orders had come straight from National Command Authority; the president of the United States declared that a clear threat to Americans and the American homeland had been detected and researched and found to be in Ethiopia, and the route taken by the planners of an attack against the US was from the Port of Bosaso inland to Addis Ababa.

The team leader for this unit, call sign Mantis One, had marveled at the extreme length the planner of this attack was taking; the distance from Bosaso—a sleepy little livestock port—to Addis Ababa was a grueling thirty-hour driving trip overland. And the area traveled was hot, dry, and dangerous. Mantis One had joined the navy because he liked water routes; this trip would be like driving the Mohave Desert. Oh well, thought the SEAL Commander, if we don't get him, the desert might.

Once they reached the port area, the pilot of the wet submersible ditched the small submarine into an alcove where it could be retrieved later. The unit of six lethal warriors, along with the pilot and navigator, moved quietly through the water together and surfaced in a layer of muck at the end of a wooden pier stem. The mix of diesel oil, plastic bags, and cattle manure made this area very unpleasant, but it would not be an area that dockworkers would search. Once the commander called in by satellite radio that his team had arrived and was in place, they spread out to find acceptable vantage points for observation while avoiding detection. No other unit in the world did this type of reconnaissance as well as the US Navy SEALs, and for them, it was just another day aboveground.

"Mantis One, this is Mantis Five," came the low signal from a team member across the port. "I have two wooden dhows full of sheep and a crew with full bladders," he reported, as he watched several small, dark men stand together and relieve themselves into the water twenty yards from his position.

"Copy that," replied Mantis One. "Any sign of the bearded Jihadi we were briefed on?"

"Negative," came the reply.

"Then keep the line clear and find the guy we were told to look for and report any suspicious traffic!"

The reissuance of orders and a slight rebuke came from the commander. He knew that complacency killed more troops than combat, and he was determined to get this team out of this shithole alive.

Chapter Twenty

27 December 1997
The Somali border with Ethiopia

Betts was not tired, but he was hungry, anxious, and frustrated. He had traveled to the border checkpoint near Borama to see over any arrivals from Somaliland that might be Al-Zedicki. As the hot breeze blew across his vantage point on a shaky metal tower overlooking the roadway, he was reminded of the Jordanian desert where he had trained local army troops in counterterrorism tactics. This breeze was much hotter than what he had felt in the Jordanian plains, and the scene of people scrambling to and from the single-room border checkpoint was much more chaotic. But the memory took him back to the attempted shooting, the prince that saved the day, and the beautiful woman unharmed by his quick action. It was all a blur, but the eventual reward of meeting her father, as well as seeing the prince again, was a respite from all the bullshit, the negativity, and the second-guessing he had endured over the last few years.

He wondered why the system was so unhelpful to the men and women who risked their lives to protect America. Why choose to be petty and thin-skinned when ordinary people were willing to perform extraordinary feats of sacrifice and service in the name of the USA? Darryl Beeker had a full career in the marine corps, but then he joined the FBI working out of the New York field office. Jim Brewer had progressed to the rank of master trooper in the Virginia State Police, but then joined the CIA to be a case officer working in Pakistan. Betts remembered a woman he had worked with in Tbilisi who had a very successful business in financial consulting but closed down her company to become a finance officer working in austere and unhealthy conditions. Why be indifferent to these people? Why turn them down for promotion or pass them over for mopes that live at headquarters? This question came to an abrupt end as his operations chief from Addis Station came running up the stairs to give him some news.

"Randy, we just got word from Africom; Al-Zedicki and several of his men were spotted at the Port of Bosaso. They're unloading large containers from a cargo ship," said the ops chief.

Africom was short for Africa Command, the central coordination center for all US military operations in central Africa. Based in Kenya, this huge facility housed command elements of each of the four branches and helped coordinate any and all US Coast Guard operations in the seas surrounding the continent. They had been instructed to support and assist Addis Station by any means feasible.

The operations chief of Addis Station, a fifteen-year veteran of the operations directorate at CIA, had been thoroughly briefed on the importance of the operation under Betts's control and was read the riot act about the consequences of not supporting him. Duly mollified and lightly threatened by the DCIA's Chief of Staff, this career intelligence officer would not threaten his tenure by talking down to Betts.

"What do we do now—wait for them to come across the border?" Betts said.

"Nope," came the happy reply. "We are going to Puntland and stop them there." The decision had been made to stop Al-Zedicki at the Bosaso Port.

"The state department is being notified, and they are coordinating with any staff members in the area. No standing embassy in Mogadishu, and we haven't recognized Puntland as a sovereign nation. So this will all be addressed at the port or as close to it as possible."

"That port is hundreds of miles away. How are we going to get there in time?" said Betts. He was computing the distance and hours of hard travel to get there.

"Again, Africom to the rescue," said the smiling ops chief.

Before Betts could ask the next question, a sound started to emanate at the horizon. The sound grew to a steady, menacing growl before any of the quizzical crowds of people in the border center could see anything. The growl grew to a whipping roar, and then the source of the sound appeared out of the southern sky.

Betts's heart lightened at the sight of two CH-47D Chinook helicopters escorted by two AH-64 Apache gunships heading to a clearing just west of the border crossing facility. Just the two Chinooks touched down, and the Apache gun ships, armed with 20-mm rotating-barrel cannons and missile pods, rose to a holding pattern of circling the amazed crowd at the border station. Not even the experienced military men among the Ethiopian Border Service had seen such a collection of machinery and ordnance.

"That's our ride!" shouted the ops chief over the sound of the two tandem-rotored birds sitting in a hot spin, ready to take on passengers and lift off.

Betts and the ops chief ran to the bird with the loadmaster standing outside the lowered ramp at the back of the helicopter. He waved them over, loaded the two men quickly onboard, and signaled to the pilot they were ready to launch.

As they rose into the air and started a full-speed jaunt to the east, Betts found himself with five men he didn't know. One was the loadmaster, an air force sergeant who was handing him and the ops chief a set of headphones to shield their ears from the incredible noise. They allowed them to communicate through the chopper's radio system.

"Welcome aboard," called the loadmaster, "It'll take us a couple of hours to get to the port, but if your guy leaves early, we'll get the word from the recon team in the area."

Betts wanted to ask who was watching the port, but he settled for thanking them for the ride.

"Thank you, I appreciate all this," he shouted into the mike. "Who's in the other Chinook?"

"Ordnance team," came the reply from the loadmaster. "The EOD guys will secure the bomb at the site and arrange for removal."

"I can't believe we got this much horsepower this quickly!" said Betts. His experience with the military was that it would take more than a week to assemble this kind of response.

"Hey," said the loadmaster, "when the daughter of the undersecretary of the army tells us to get in the air, we only ask about the altitude."

"Who?" Betts was a bit confused by this statement.

"Olivia Johnson. We used to call her OJ when she worked psych ops, because with a little bit of training and the right motivation, she might kill anybody!" joked the loadmaster.

Betts was amazed. He had not known about the DCIA being related to a senior officer at the Pentagon, much less her work with psychological operations.

"Never knew she was army," said one of the four other men riding in the chopper. "You think she'd have gotten us a better ride."

Betts turned to the man who said this. He was solid and seriously buff, slightly bigger and younger than the rest. Betts bent at the waist and spoke into the mike, directly into the younger man's face as he pointed to the floor of the Chinook.

"This is the finest helicopter ever made. It is faster than any Huey or Blackhawk, carries more weight than a couple of tractor trailers, and rides as smooth as a baby's bottom!"

Betts's time in the marine corps included many trips in such a marvelous bird, and he was sorry to hear that the service life of these incredible machines would be ending in favor of a different dual-rotor thing they called an Osprey.

"We haven't met," responded the younger man with neither guile nor regret. "Mark Trout, Office of Security Protective Ops Cadre. We are your shadows for this thing; these guys are my Cobra team. We have been briefed on the op and hope that we can get this thing settled quick fast and in a hurry. Those are our instructions from OJ!"

He motioned to the other men with him, who were all dressed out in level three armored vests with a chest rig holding spare ammo magazines. They carried Glock sidearms and M-4 rifles with Eotech holographic sights. The helmets they wore were military-standard and fitted with flip-down night-vision goggles. They were not the same as a platoon of FAST marines, but they appeared to be just as well-armed and coiled to strike.

"Good to have you," Betts said loudly to the Cobra team. "Look, I may have a man on the ground there, as asset who has given us all this info. You would be able to recognize him by his slightly lighter hair than the others, but please hold off on shooting everybody right away!"

The Cobra team, an experienced team of CIA protective officers, regarded this information for a moment, and then Mark Trout spoke again.

"Fair enough! The only target we've been told about is the leader of this bunch, Al-Zeedeck!" Trout mispronounced. "So we have no word on any other threats. But when we get there, and people are shooting at us, they have to go!"

As Betts was nodding, understanding of this, the radio crackled with another voice, one from the cockpit.

"We're getting word that the target group is splitting up! A bunch of guys in a Bongo van full of weapons and gear just left the port heading west."

Betts leaned toward the front of the long, dark fuselage.

"Do we know who? Any descriptions of who's in the truck?"

The pilot looked annoyed to have to relay this information.

"Negative, all the boys in the water are saying is that the bearded guy and some kid stayed behind."

This meant Al-Zedicki was still at the port; he may have sent the others ahead to scout the terrain and advise if the border crossing was closed or under any scrutiny.

"There goes our escort," called the ops chief from Addis. As Betts turned to see out the window, he saw the two Apache gunships tilt off and head straight to the south, toward Kenya.

"They were just to get us safely into Puntland before the advisements were done. Them leaving means that the state department got word to the local government about who we were and not to mess with us," said the loadmaster.

Betts watched them disappear, as he dreaded what was coming up. This was going to be a firefight. Al-Zedicki would have planned for this, and he would take anyone down that threatened his attack plans. Betts hoped that Munir would be clear of all this upcoming carnage.

Chapter Twenty-One

27 December 1997
Port of Bosaso

At the same time that Betts and his armed team were speeding east at 180 miles per hour toward the port, Al-Zedicki was giving instructions to his team on their mission as they were piling guns, ammunition, and RPG-7 rocket launchers into the large unmarked white Bongo van that had brought them here. This vehicle had been rented by Al-Zedicki weeks before, and it was now parked in a large steel shed at the eastern edge of the port facility. The only other thing left in the cavernous shed was a three-ton dump truck that now held a large steel container that had been lifted from the container ship that Al-Zedicki was preoccupied with. Placement of the container on the bed of the dump truck was precarious, as the end of the large metal box extended over the end of the lowered tailgate by about a foot. The container barely fit onto the bed of the large truck, but it had been securely locked down and could possibly survive the trip to Addis Ababa. The truck was then backed into the large metal shed.

The weapons and gear had been sealed into the other large container lifted off the cargo ship. This was a standard shipping container, almost ten meters long and tall enough to stand in upright. It now sat at the edge of the concrete pier, doors open to display a simple wooden container. Anyone could look inside the container, but the remaining guns, ammo, and rocket launchers were locked away in the large wooden box inside. Those two containers were all that was on the ship, and the crew had been paid. But rather than untether their boat and leave the dock, the crew of seventeen men took part in unpacking and checking the large number of rifles and gear in the second container.

"Those are my secondary team," Al-Zedicki said to Munir as he waved goodbye to the Bongo van as it left the port. Al-Araaj and the others had piled in and taken off without a word. "Those men that you worked with—they know Addis Ababa very well, and they will scout out the return route for the dump truck!"

"Secondary team?" said Munir, troubled by the layers and extensive planning undertaken by this terrorist mastermind.

"The crew have been paid to stay here and make sure that the truck gets out of the port safely. Once the truck is gone and no longer under the thumb of the port authority, they can keep their guns and leave with the ship."

"We are driving to Addis in that thing?" Munir asked as he pointed at the large, ungainly truck that appeared to be straining under the weight of the container it carried.

"You are driving the truck. I am following you in a sedan that I have parked in the outer lot," Al-Zedicki said, smiling. "Don't worry, the device cannot explode without a call from the cell phone I'll be carrying!"

Munir paused to look at this slippery criminal; he had laid out a fairly complex plan of moving parts and deadly intentions. The bomb in the container weighed more than one ton and would not fit in the van that the crew had worked so hard to customize. It must have been another part of his plan that he was willing to sacrifice— all the planning and gathering and waiting and risking exposure to the authorities. All for nothing, he was going to have Munir drive this thing through the border and right up to the embassy and set it off remotely. A simple plan obfuscated by complex preparations.

Chapter Twenty-Two

27 December 1997
South of Erigamo, Puntland, 100 miles west of the Port of Bosaso

"Looks like it," called the copilot from the CH-47's cockpit. The helicopter slowed from its mad dash toward the port and tilted at an angle that allowed everyone to see the ground under them.

Everyone in the fuselage craned to get a look out of the windows. Betts saw that the sole vehicle on the road right now was a bulbous white van bouncing along the dirt road below them. Several faces from inside the van were looking up at the two menacing machines that had suddenly slowed to a hover. For a moment, everyone in the van was staring at everyone in the helicopter and vice versa.

Then the van stopped. As the helicopter carrying the passengers stayed in a hover to look over the white van, the second Chinook took a station above and to the right. They were keeping an eye over the entire scene.

"Is that your boy in that van?" the pilot asked.

"I can't see him. It doesn't mean he's not in there; I just can't see them very well," Betts responded.

"I can get you a bit closer, or we can land. It's just that… Wait, hold up!"

The pilot suddenly jerked his bird to the left as he switched channels to the other helicopter.

Betts and the others saw the rear doors of the white van open and two men climb out holding weapons. One was holding an AK-47 and taking a straight aim at him. The other man was holding a Russian RPG-7a rocket launcher as a third man scrambled out of the van with a rocket to load into the launcher.

"Never mind," said the pilot calmly. "We're outa here."

And the Chinook took a steep move higher into the air and arched away to the north.

As Betts was twisting in his seat and trying to see if the any of the men outside the van were Munir, the white van disappeared in a cloud of churned-up dirt, flame, and smoke. The hollow whoosh of the 70-mm rocket pods was followed by the thunderous clap of the secondary explosion and was felt by everyone inside the helicopter. As the Chinook carrying Betts and the others turned into a tight circle to look at the demolition, the second Chinook took a low straight pass over the site.

"Okay, the other bird took out the shooters. What do you wanna do? It's safe to land if you wanna check for your boy," the pilot said matter-of-factly.

"Shit no, head for the port," the sudden and impatient voice of the Addis ops chief said. "Sorry Betts, but the bomb and Al-Zedicki are the mission, and that wasn't either of them."

Betts nodded, suddenly overwhelmed by the sight of the strike. He had heard before about CH-47s being armed with rocket pods, but he had never seen one in action. As the two Chinooks resumed their trip east at full speed, Betts hoped that Munir wasn't in that van.

Chapter Twenty-three

27 December 1997
Port of Bosaso

Al-Zedicki was aggravated. The phone call he received from the four men in the Bongo van rang once, and then ended without connecting. They had been underway for two hours, and the phone call was unexpected. Al-Zedicki's efforts to return the call were unsuccessful. Damned desert had no cellular service.

"Open the back of the container. I want to make sure the battery on the device is charged and ready," Al-Zedicki said to Munir.

Munir walked through the large shed to the back of the container resting on the bed of the truck and looked at the lock securing the doors. Hanging from the lock was a key ring attached to the key in the lock. Munir climbed up on the bed, stepped around the back of the container to the locked door, and took the key out of the lock. He slipped it into his shoe and called around the edge to Al-Zedicki.

"It's locked. Do you have the key?"

Al-Zedicki was staring at Munir as he walked forward out of the shed. Munir was gambling that all the preparations and assembling undertaken by Al-Zedicki had distracted him from focusing on the lock that secured the container. Munir saw him turn quickly and shout questions at the crewmen who were standing around or sitting under a nearby fever tree. They responded in a variety of languages, mostly with no recognition or simply shrugging their shoulders. Al-Zedicki added impatience to his aggravation and sent several men back onto the rusting hulk at the dock to search for keys. When they didn't immediately reappear, one of the crewmen walked through the shed to the back of the truck while holding a Tokarev A-100 rifle. This was a semiautomatic Russian weapon that

159

held eight 7.62x54-mm rounds, heavy bullets that carved deep holes in anything they hit. When he pointed the ancient-but-accurate rifle at the lock on the container door, Al-Zedicki screamed for him to stop and sent him scurrying away. Using a 30-caliber weapon to shoot the lock off a container holding one thousand kilograms of high explosives was a poor choice.

"Go on the boat and find me some tools. Get a file or chan-nel-locks," Al-Zedicki commanded Munir. This was going to delay the departure for awhile. Munir walked slowly to the boat, careful not to dislodge the key from within his shoe. He wasn't sure if he was accomplishing anything by delaying Al-Zedicki, other than postponing the plans for his death.

Chapter Twenty-Four

27 December 1997
The Port of Bosaso

"Mantis One, this is Mantis Two. I've lost my line of sight. A new boat came in, and it's blocking my view. I'm moving to a new spot." Mantis Two was the communications link with Africom, and his ability to report what was happening to the central command in Kenya was essential to this mission.

"Roger Mantis Two, but keep low," the commander said. He couldn't see the area where the bearded guy and the kid were, but he was close to the bow end of the old container ship that had brought the two containers. As he watched the crew, who were now armed with a variety of rifles, come and go onto the ship, he thought about getting a review of his team's location.

"Team, I need an update. What do you see and is your location secure?" Mantis One said.

His information was that the EOD team and extra shooters were inbound and less than an hour out. If they needed to move up and support the EOD team, they had small arms that would work to suppress any threats to the choppers. If they needed to remove themselves from the area, stealth was going to be important. He wanted to make sure everyone was in the right place.

"This is Three. I'm on the north end, about one hundred yards away from the boat. I'm watching cattle, kids, and port cops."

"This is Four. I'm at the entrance to the port, watching for anything coming in that might be aligned with the bearded guy."

"This is Five. I'm across the port entrance from Four. I've got eyes on the boat and the crew on the dock. I'm seeing a lot of hardware here but nothing organized."

The team leader waited. He knew that his second man was moving to a new location, but he heard nothing from him at the end of this radio check. The communications officer was out of position and not reporting.

"Mantis Two, are you settled yet?"

Nothing.

"Does anyone have eyes on Mantis Two?"

"Boss, this is Three. I've got some excited dock workers telling a port cop something. They're moving south toward you."

Mantis One took a fresh look at his purview. He had a sliver of a view of the dock but not much else. He heard someone calling out in a shout, and then he heard the same words shouted again.

"Mantis Two, contact!"

The loud, quick message came over the radio. Everyone froze in position. Mantis Two had either been discovered or was in contact with a threat.

Suddenly the busy port became a hive of new activity. People were running in both directions in and out of the immediate offloading area. Shouts and frantic splashing in the water told the team leader that his man was in trouble, but he couldn't risk all his team's profile just yet.

"Mantis Four and Five, move to my location on the south side at the bow of the container ship. Mantis Three, keep your location. Can you see anything of Two?"

He was consolidating his team in case they needed to remove his second man from the area.

And then came the shot. The crack of a rifle round, possibly an AK-47, was followed by more shots and shouts as dock workers and the crew of the container ship started shooting into the water just beyond the bow of the container ship.

"This is One. Can anyone see what or who they are shooting at?"

"Mantis One, all I see is guys pointing into the water and some shooting."

"Okay team, change of plans. Everybody move to the dock, find a target, and start taking out anybody with a gun. Mantis Two is out of touch and may be down. Move to the dock and get some!" Mantis Team didn't start this firefight, but they were sure as hell were going to end it.

Then came a startled voice crackling onto the radio net, "This is Mantis Two! I'm fine! A steer fell off the dock onto my location, and they just started shooting at it! I say again, I'm fine, and I'm secure!"

The team leader took a second to process this.

"Team, return to your location, stay low. Do not engage; do not engage. Mantis Two, did you say a steer fell on you?"

"It came off the dock and landed right above me! I've never seen anything with horns that big that close to me. It was thrashing and trying to get upright, and I guess they don't have a way to lift it out, so they just started shooting the poor thing. Once one guy fired, a bunch of armed guys showed up and joined in!"

"Okay team, return to your locations."

Mantis One drew a deep breath and tried to relax.

The shooting and shouts down the shoreline from Al-Zedicki's position added to his panic. As he watched the excited crowd pointing into the water, he heard one man fire a shot, which was joined by other men shooting into the water. When Al-Zedicki saw that some of his crew had joined this madness, he called out to them, shouting for them to get back to the boat.

Then a uniformed Port Authority policeman approached and started asking the crew members about their guns. This was getting ugly fast.

As Munir was coming back from the boat, he heard the shots and looked over to see a small crowd pointing fingers and rifles into the water's edge. He had found a large, flat-iron file that might be able to work against the hasp holding the lock. This would take a while, but it could help delay getting access to the back of the container.

Al-Zedicki came running up to him and demanded that he get to the shed where the truck was sitting. Munir tried to tell him that he was heading that way now. The terrorist leader was now a mumbling mass of panic. He ran screaming to where the crewmen were standing and started pushing them toward the shed also. It was obvious that this plan was falling apart; Al-Zedicki was trying to get his men away from the policeman, who was questioning two members of the crew about their rifles.

And then a low sound started growing around them, rising to just a bit louder than the noise of the dock machinery. As people working the dock stopped what they were doing, the sound increased. It became a flat, whipping roar before they could see two large helicopters approaching from the west.

As Munir and a dozen of the crewmen assembled in front of the dump truck, Al-Zedicki ran up, grabbed Munir by the arm, and led him to the first container, which still laid open. Al-Zedicki opened the wooden storage box that held the weapons and handed Munir an RPG-7 rocket launcher.

"What am I going to do with this?" Munir said. He had not touched one since his brief training in Pakistan, and this ungainly thing would create more problems than it would solve. The instructors told Munir that the firing of the grenade from the launcher would immediately give away his position, so the smart thing was to fire and run for a different location.

As Al-Zedicki was reaching in to retrieve two rockets for Munir, he said, "You need to draw their fire! Run to the back of the boat and take out those helicopters! Don't let them get to the truck; the crewmen and I will fire at them to keep them from shooting you, and you take them out with the rockets!"

With this said, he handed the two 40-mm rockets to Munir and pushed him in the direction of the boat. Once he looked at the rockets, Munir recognized that they were the type of grenade that would explode upon impact. This was a not an armor-piercing grenade; instead it was a fairly unstable and clumsy rocket that could kill the operator as well as the target.

Munir knew this was last-minute madness. A military response was coming to the port, most likely to stop this plot. Al-Zedicki was trying to save the truck, and the best way to do that was to draw the fire of the helicopters. Munir, like so many other young men he had met, was being sacrificed for the goals and ambitions of an evil plotter.

He turned from Al-Zedicki and started running. As he ran toward the stern end of the container ship, he began to load the rocket into the launcher. He ran as far as his lungs would allow; he was separated from the truck inside the metal shed, then he heard the thunderous noise change slightly, and he stopped. Munir looked up to see two huge green aircraft hovering just four hundred feet from where he stood. They seemed to be looking right at him. These were Americans, and they had come to kill or be killed. Munir was over 150 yards from the truck and staring at two huge, hovering shapes that foretold death and destruction.

Munir held the loaded RPG-7 down at his right side as he used his left hand to reach under his shirt and bring out his faded canteen. Once it was out and hanging free around his neck, he raised the rocket launcher and held the second grip with his left hand. He took off the safety.

"That's Munir!" Betts shouted into the helicopter's mike. "That's my guy!"

"That's an RPG," came the voice of the pilot. "And we didn't come all this way to get shot out of the sky!"

"WAIT!" Betts screamed.

"What the hell?" someone said into their headset.

The two helicopter crews stood motionless, one hundred feet apart, as the young man with the RPG-7 turned suddenly to his left and fired his rocket into a large, corrugated metal shed that was crowded with armed men. The rocket traveled at 120 yards per second, leaving a white smoke trail that headed into the shed and hit something solid. The explosion was beyond anything the pilots were expecting. The metal shed flew apart in a blinding gush of fire and smoke, and the blast pushed both birds back several feet in the air as the pilots struggled to stay steady. Even at 150 yards away, the blast blew Munir off his feet and onto the very edge of the dock. The launcher and second grenade splashed into the water. Munir was dazed and cut with shrapnel, but he was alive.

The EOD helicopter once again moved higher and farther back. They were adopting an overview and radioing everything to Africom. This scene had gone from dangerous to bizarre, and anything could happen now.

The bird carrying Betts and the POC team landed, and as everyone scrambled out the back of the spinning machine, Munir struggled to his feet and stared at the flaming hulk that had been a real threat just seconds before. Munir couldn't hear the screams of the men blown from the building and burning, or the flaming fuel, or even the monstrous whine of the helicopters. He had been deafened by the blast, and all he could do now was stare and stumble a bit as sheets of metal and flaming chunks fell all around him.

And then Betts was there. He ran up and grabbed Munir and hugged him close as he said all kinds of things that Munir could not hear. But Betts was there, and he was smiling. .

Then Munir noticed something strange. A small team of armed

men had surrounded him and Betts. They were facing out, away from him, holding their rifles against their chest and watching. They were keeping anyone from getting to him and Betts. Most of the dock workers had fled the scene of the explosion, but a few were curious about this unbelievable explosion, and they were anxious to find out what was happening. These Americans were protecting them from the gathering crowd. Protecting him and Betts. For the first time in his life, Munir did not feel like an outcast.

Chapter Twenty-five

Two months later, 1 March 1998
The rooftop of the Mclean Hilton Hotel, Tysons Corner, Virginia

It had taken some convincing, but the hotel management had finally relented and allowed the two government workers access to the roof area. As long as no food, drinks, or tobacco were brought up there, Betts and Brewer could sit there and watch the sunset.

As Brewer carefully retrieved his flask of Four Branches bourbon from his hip pocket, Betts lit up two cigars and handed one to him. The two men gave a quick toast to a better life, and then settled into their folding chaise lounges and admired the traffic, the lights, and the diminishing day. It was cold up here, and both men held their jackets tight against them to ward off the chilly breeze.

"Thanks again for calling me. How'd your flight in go?" Betts asked as he took a small sip of the finely crafted Tennessee product from the metal flask.

"Fine. They gave me a week to come back for a class, so I thought of looking you up," Brewer said. He retrieved his flask from Betts's grip and took a swig of his own.

"Munir get home all right? I know he was anxious to get back to his folks."

Betts had arranged for Munir to come back to Addis with him from the Port of Bosaso; they just had to land and wait for an MC-130 aerial tanker to arrive from Kenya for a refuel. The two Chinooks had used up their fuel getting to the port at that speed, and Africa Command was quick to arrange for a safe return.

Once in Addis, Munir was flown to Islamabad where the US State Department wanted to congratulate him and start the paperwork for getting him the reward for volunteering information that led to the end of the threat posed by Hafez Al-Zedicki. It wasn't every day that the US government handed out $5 million from the Counter-Terrorist Reward Program, so this would take a while to sort out.

The chief of station in Islamabad arranged for safe travel to Chitral by way of an MI-17 helicopter flown by the Pakistani army. The Inter-Services and Intelligence Directorate had offered to take Munir to his home, but the offer had been refused. ISID was still upset about a missing investigator from the Frontier Region, and COS Islamabad was eager to keep Munir away from any questioning they might have. Using a bird from the Pakistani military helped keep the ISID investigators away from Munir for the moment.

"He looked happy when we landed at Chitral," Brewer said. He had stayed with Munir to see him safe all the way home. Munir's family was there when they landed, and Brewer watched Munir's mother and father clutch him tightly as they walked away. The three of them only stopped hugging and walking together when they arrived where a fourth person was standing. The tall, slender form of Munir's brother Azzam reached out to grab Munir close to him and kiss him on each cheek. They exchanged a few words, and then the four of them walked to their new vehicle, a used Range Rover that nobody claimed.

"I'd like to go out there someday, see that place, see Munir. Meet that amazing family," Betts said as he gazed into the darkening horizon.

It was then that Brewer opened his jacket enough to reach in and bring something out.

"He told me to give you this."

Brewer handed a canteen to Betts. It had a faded wool covering and the beads were less colorful than they had once been. The seams of the wool covering were coming apart, and the rope had come loose on one end, but it was the most powerful, beautiful gift he had ever been given.

"Thank you, partner," Betts said as he admired the weathered pouch through watery eyes. It made everything worth it.

Epilogue

Although this story is fiction, the terrorist attacks of this time frame were factual. The overseas threat posed by committed terrorists has been acknowledged for some time, but the will to face up to the cost of keeping dedicated representatives of the military, the foreign service, and the intelligence community who work to keep our country safe is an elusive one.

"A careful examination of the nature and frequency of terrorism, civil strife, urban violence, and comparable occurrences throughout the world has led the Panel to recommend that a large number of facilities around the world, which once may have represented the optimal site for the conduct of American diplomacy, be replaced by more physically secure sites and buildings. The Panel believes that it is essential that a substantial relocation and building program be initiated and carried out with dispatch. The alternative is to remain hostage to the likelihood of American diplomatic establishments being physically assaulted by mobs or bombed or sabotaged by terrorists. This building program should be undertaken as rapidly as possible and should be sustained until it is completed. To accomplish this, adequate, continuing, secured funding must be assured. The Panel recommends a capital budgeting system that will permit progress at the maximum feasible pace." — The Inman Report on Embassy Security and Safety, 1985.

On 7 August 1998, the US embassies in Nairobi, Kenya and Dar Es' Salam, Tanzania were blown up by Al-Qaeda operatives under the orders of Osama Bin Laden. Over 220 people were killed and almost 5,000 injured, most of them indigenous workers serving the US government. The blasts from the truck bombs were suicide attacks coordinated to explode almost simultaneously, using a combination of TNT, ammonium nitrate, and det cord.

Osama Bin Laden's fatwas against the West, one in 1996 and the other in 1998, were well known to the intelligence community but considered empty threats by politicians in Washington, DC. Although the Inman Report, quoted above, pointed out the safety deficiencies and security upgrades necessary for all overseas embassies, they were not implemented at the "maximum feasible pace" recommended.

"Only the enemy shows you where you are weak. Only the enemy tells you where he is strong. And the rules of the game are what you can do to him and what you can stop him from doing to you."

Author Unknown

Acknowledgments

I want to acknowledge the help of Bob and Karin Schlesinger, author John Racoosin, and my lovely wife Debbie. They have helped me enormously.

About the Author

This work is fiction, but the enormous amount of work that goes into supporting those who volunteer to defend this country and represent its interests is a fact. The United States is represented by DOD men and women and state department foreign service officers who strive to make the world better. But the US is also guarded by another army, a select group of men and women who wear no uniform, who sometimes carry a weapon for self-defense, and who meet with characters both famous and unsavory. They gather information from people that would make you cross the street if you saw them walking toward you on the sidewalk. They do this to collect valuable information that policy makers desperately need to make informed decisions about the US' policies abroad. I served in this capacity for almost two decades, and I was honored to have worked with some of the best officers that ever represented this country. They are a rare, dedicated breed of citizens who strive to avoid American blindness overseas, and the US population knows little about their work. Not even close family members are aware of their sacrifice. That's okay; those who have done this work know how to thank them.

Milton Keynes UK
Ingram Content Group UK Ltd.
UKHW020701040324
438885UK00018B/1174